Expectation

Ghost Targets, Volume 2

Aaron Pogue

Published by Masked Fox Productions, 2011.

EXPECTATION

First edition. February 15, 2011.

Copyright © 2011 Aaron Pogue.

ISBN: 978-1936559084

Written by Aaron Pogue.

Also by Aaron Pogue

A Consortium of Worlds
A Consortium of Worlds No. 1
A Consortium of Worlds No. 2

A Dragonswarm Short Story
Remnant
From Embers

Auric's Valiants
Notes from a Thief
Auric and the Wolf

Ghost Targets
Surveillance
Expectation
Restraint
Camouflage

The Dragonprince's Arrows
A Darkness in the East

The Dragonprince's Legacy
Taming Fire
The Dragonswarm
The Dragonprince's Heir
The Original Dragonprince Trilogy

Unstressed Syllables Presents
Turn Your Story into an eBook: Easy Self-Publishing with
Draft2Digital.com

Watch for more at AaronPogue.com.

Prologue

He hit her, before he died, and that made it just a little easier. It wasn't much of a strike, just wild flailing, but his class ring split the skin above her right eyebrow. She heard the sickening sound of it biting into the bony ridge above her eye, accompanied by a blinding flash of pain. She shook it off a moment later and caught at his wrist. For an instant their fingers closed together, like lovers holding hands, then she put her weight on his arm and pressed it down to the floor, careful not to bruise him with the effort. His other arm was pinned under his body, and she was clear of his thrashing legs.

As she surveyed him, her eyes fell on his for one horrifying moment. His were too wide, rolling like those of a panicked horse, and she could imagine all too easily the confusion and fear and betrayal exploding in his brain. The pain, too. A tear slipped from her eye. But there was nothing available that could do what she needed without causing pain. She ripped her gaze away and mouthed *I'm sorry* to the cold floor. He couldn't see her face now, but it didn't matter. It would be over soon.

She almost screamed when his watch started beeping, a futile alarm as the watch's face began to burn an angry red. She bit back her yell, though, calling herself all kinds of silly. She'd known the alarm was coming.

How much time had passed? She glanced at her own wrist, where a stopwatch whizzed merrily through the microseconds. Only a few seconds had passed. Disbelief froze her for a moment, but her preparations finally overwhelmed her surprise, and she forced herself to pay attention to the numbers on her watch. To understand them.

Only eight seconds; two since the alarm had gone off. Three now. She had four seconds left, and if it wasn't done by the time her clock hit twelve, she was dead, too. Thousandths of a second flew, like grains of sand hurtling through the gap in an hourglass. Too quickly, she thought, glancing once more at his face, then tearing her eyes away. The stopwatch felt malicious somehow, acting out his vengeance. The imaginary sand was determined to bury her. Thousandths and hundredths and tenths of a second flew by, ripping away her chance of escape. The seconds slipped away, but still it felt like an age. Waiting, not knowing.

Her watch said 0:00:10.271 when his watch beeped once, a benign sound announcing a false alarm, and the backlight switched back from red to white. All clear. His body was still now, on the floor, his head twisted around at a strange angle and his eyes mercifully closed. His chest rose and fell, slow, rhythmic, but he was gone. She kept her eyes locked on his watch for another minute, but it showed only the Mountain Standard Time with an abbreviated weather report in a smaller font below. Hippocrates didn't know. She took a deep breath and let it out. No alarm from Hippocrates, and God knew there were no cameras in the lab. That meant there were no emergency sirens screaming toward the clinic, no reports generating in Jurisprudence, no cops setting up roadblocks at a two-mile perimeter from the scene of the crime. She took another deep breath, and felt her fear escape her as she exhaled. There was no crime, only a tragedy. Only an accident.

Her fear dissolved, leaving behind only pity. She caught his hand, raised it as though to kiss it, but instead slipped the bloody class ring off his finger. Her forehead burned where he'd hit her, but it hadn't bled much. She let his hand fall, rose gracefully, and looked down on his still form for some time. "I'm sorry," she said, then disappeared into the night.

1. Back to Work

Katie couldn't help glancing up at the security camera, but she immediately tore her gaze away. "This is my job," she mumbled under her breath. She fixed her attention on her own dull reflection in the elevator doors instead. A little small for a federal agent, but she packed a punch. She'd ridden up this elevator twelve times before—before fleeing to South America in hot pursuit of a villain and then spending weeks in a hospital there. Her hair was back to its natural black after that trip, and starting to grow out long again. In stark contrast, her skin looked awfully pale. The convalescence had been a tough one.

Less than a week on the job and over a month away from it, and, riding up now, she had no idea what to expect at the top. Lucky number thirteen, she thought, and her eyes drifted back up to the camera. Her hands clenched and relaxed, again and again in her nervousness.

She tore her eyes away again and told herself again, more firmly this time, "This is my job."

A bell chimed at her floor, and when the doors flew back, Reed was there, looming right in the doorway. Behind him were the crystal clear, bulletproof glass doors with the words "Ghost Targets" frosted into them at eye level. In her time away, she had imagined a hundred different ways this could go, and the ones with Reed waiting for her at the elevator all went bad. In real life, it was even more terrifying, and she had to bite back a frightened little yelp.

Reed merely took a short step into the elevator, nose-to-nose with Katie even as she fell back a pace, and without looking he punched the button for the ground floor. She remembered Reed, tall and lithe and in charge. He smelled like fresh soap and quiet strength. She expected him to take her shoulders, to restrain her against whatever he had to say, but he pinned her in place with just a look.

At last he spoke, his voice kinder than anything she'd ever heard from Rick. "This *is* your job."

She nodded, and realized to her horror she was close to tears.

Reed pulled back to arm's length without releasing her eyes. "Katie, what are you doing here?" He saw her fear then, and his face softened. "Oh, Katie, don't get me wrong." His shoulders slumped, and for a moment he looked like a little boy who'd made a big mistake. "You are absolutely welcome here, Katie. Hell, you're *needed* here, right now, but you should be at home getting rest—"

"I've rested enough," she said, her chin coming up with more defiance than she really felt. "Reed, I need to do something. I'm going nuts, trapped at home alone. I need to be back on the job."

Before he answered, the doors chimed open on the lobby. She imagined him shoving her back out, shouting after her to go home, and for a heartbeat she could see the same scenario playing out in his eyes. Then, without ever breaking eye contact, he punched the button for their office. "Fine," he said, "but I'm keeping an eye on you. You've got nothing to prove, Katie, and we need you healthy, got it?"

She nodded, somewhat cowed, and he finally stepped off to the side, staring at the elevator doors instead of her.

"How much do you know?" he said.

"What?"

"You've been cleared with Craig for a week and a half now. Thought you might want to get up to speed while you convalesced."

She rounded on him, all her earlier timidity lost in a flash of frustration. "Why didn't you tell me? I could have been working all this time? Dammit, Reed—"

He laughed, which startled her enough to break her tirade. She blinked, then asked more quietly, "Why didn't you tell me?"

He clapped her on the shoulder. "You were half-dead, Katie. Like I said, we need you healthy up here. We were never really flush to begin with, and losing Rick... God, no matter what he was, losing Rick is a real blow." He trailed off, silent for a moment, then shook it off. "I didn't message you, because I was worried you would take the news as an assignment and push yourself too far too fast."

She shrugged, knowing her presence here just confirmed that to him. He didn't drive the point home. Instead, he turned back to business. "Well, ever since word of Rick's duplicity got out, the Government Accountability Office has been all over us. They're reviewing all our active cases from the last year, and that's put a real limit on what we can do."

The doors flew open once more on their offices, and he called over his headset, "Craig, let us in. Thanks."

Katie frowned. "So...."

"So my hands are tied for the moment when it comes to existing cases, which frees me up to take on a new one. You and me, I should say." He stepped past her and caught the open door, holding it for her, and as she stepped into the office, everything he was saying slipped from Katie's mind.

She hadn't been back since the night she shot out a window and took her chance with the building's fire escape. A shudder caught her as she stepped across the threshold and into the office where she'd been a prisoner, if only for a few minutes.

She looked around the room. The window over her desk was already replaced, the mess of it cleaned up, and the other agents in the office were too busy at their desks to even look up at her entrance. She'd feared suspicious stares and narrowed eyes—and secretly hoped for cheers and applause. She had saved Hathor, after all, and with it the world as they knew it. But Reed was probably the only one here who knew the full story. Or maybe they all did, and that sort of thing was just commonplace for these guys. She didn't know enough to guess which it was.

Reed brought her back to the moment with a quick tap on the shoulder. "Right, then," he said. "We've got to introduce you to Dimms."

Her eyes went wide. "A new boss already?"

He laughed openly at that. "No. No. Things being what they are, finding a replacement for Rick could take months. Meantime, I'm acting department head."

"Congratulations!" she said brightly, but he didn't even smile.

He just said, "Thanks," deadpan, then nothing else as he wove his way through the desks of the bullpen. Katie almost bumped into him when he stopped abruptly at the second desk past the conference room. He put his smile back on as he made introductions. "Katie, this is Brian Dimms, one of our analysts. Brian, this is Katie Pratt—our big hero."

She didn't have to blush at that, because Brian grinned like it was a joke. That settled that, she thought. For his part, Brian was probably five foot six, early thirties, with thin red hair and a prominent nose. He had a weak chin, too, but when he turned his smile on her she took an immediate liking to him.

"Pleased to meet you, Miss Pratt!" He stuck out a hand without rising, and she shook it briskly. "Are you going to be working the Gevia case with Reed?"

"She is," Reed said as he pulled a buzzing handheld from his pocket and skimmed a new message. He sighed. "Fill her in, would you? I've got to take another meeting with the Steves."

He started to go, but caught the sudden look of fear in Katie's eyes. She felt a powerful deja vu, and it was nothing she ever wanted to go through again. But Reed shattered the memory of Rick with a look of perfect sympathy. He stepped close and lowered his voice just for her. "I'm with you on this. All the way." He held her eyes until she nodded, and then he stepped back and said firmly, "Tell her everything she wants to know, Brian." He held Katie's eyes for a moment longer, making wordless promises, then finally turned and disappeared into Rick's old office.

They both watched him go, and when Brian turned back to Katie, she realized he was nervous, unsure how to begin.

She broke the ice. "So, what's an analyst do?"

Brian blinked in surprise, then shrugged. "Up here, we watch programs that watch Hathor so cases don't take us by surprise. It was—" he jerked a thumb over his shoulder rather than say Goodall's name. "It was one of the old man's plans, because every case is urgent by the time we learn of it through official channels, and we are *always* underfunded."

He leaned back and glanced down at the open casefile on his desk. "There's patterns in the database, though—fingerprints that show up when somebody starts ghosting. The Gevia case is interesting, because the crime was already in a restricted area, but somebody has been ghosting some minor details after the fact anyway." He met her eyes with a fascinated grin. "And that somebody is the US Army."

Katie shook her head. "I don't get it."

Brian said, "Craig, get Katie a copy of the Gevia casefile. Thanks." He closed the casefile on his own desktop and instead drew up location details on the De Grey Clinic, a medical research facility in Boulder, Colorado. "Gevia is—"

"The wonder drug, I know," she said, bending over the desk to skim the site profile for the clinic. "Did it kill someone?"

"Hah! No." She looked at him, surprised, and he shrugged. "Nobody's dead, actually, but the lead researcher—the nation's only real expert on the drug—is in a coma, and it doesn't look like he's coming out of it."

"Wow," Katie said. "Oh, wow, that's terrible."

"There's no real sign one way or the other of foul play— nothing obvious in his genome to trigger an attack, but also no real signs of a struggle or any physical damage to his person. The army has called it natural causes, and they're doing everything they can to keep it quiet."

Katie held up a finger to cut him short and said, "Wait, what's the army got to do with it?"

He sucked in a deep breath and let it out slowly. "Gevia is currently classified a national resource. It was developed primarily with DoD funding, and since its commercial release it has been under tight security control by the army. That's why the clinic is a restricted area." At her blank look, he clarified. "Off-the-radar. Hathor-blind. The Aggregators get no data from the site, and the army has a special team tasked with keeping the records clean."

She whistled, impressed. "I didn't know the government had the balls to try something like that."

Brian shrugged. "They don't. *We* don't, even. DoD is another matter, though. Still, there's maybe a dozen officially restricted areas *total*. For the most part, it's more trouble than it's worth."

"But Gevia's special."

He chuckled. "There's an understatement. I don't know about you, but I was really starting to like the idea of living forever."

"So the army wants us to—"

"Oh, no, no, no. They're quite satisfied with their examiner's report. All they want is to keep this incident out of the news."

Katie sighed. "It's the family, then? Some grieving widow digging for the truth?" Brian shook his head again, and Katie frowned. "Then why are we getting involved?"

Brian chewed his lip for a moment before answering. "Well, the local police chief is raising a stink, claiming it was no accident. Seems she's never been terribly fond of the army's big black hole in the middle of her town, and she's looking to get some media attention on this to push them out. Reed thought maybe if we went in and put an official stamp on things, that would smooth things over down there."

Something about his demeanor said that wasn't the whole story, so Katie pressed him. "What else?"

"Frankly..." He glanced over his shoulder to Goodall's old office, where Reed was still meeting with the GAO investigators, though he seemed more interested in something on his handheld than whatever the investigators were saying. Brian turned back to Katie and lowered his voice anyway. "I think Reed is looking for an excuse to get out of here."

While Katie was still considering that, a memo window appeared on Brian's desktop. Under the bureau letterhead it said in block text, "Stick to the facts, would you, Dimms? Thanks.— Reed." Brian grinned sheepishly, then dismissed the memo and brought back the casefile.

"Actually," Katie said, as Brian changed to another tab, "I don't want to waste your time going over stuff that's already written down." She pulled out her handheld and verified her access to the casefile with a quick nod. "I'll get back with you once I have more questions, okay?"

"Oh, sure," he said, a hint of disappointment dragging his eyes down. "I've just—yeah, I have other stuff I can work on."

"Perfect." She turned her back on him and headed toward her old desk in the corner. On the second step in that direction, her heart started beating faster. She took a breath, willing herself to calm down, and said quietly into her headset, "Craig, is desk twelve available for use? Details to my handheld. Thanks."

She blinked in surprise when she found the first entry for the desk said, "Assigned: Katie Pratt." She reached the desk and tapped it to wake it up as she sank down into the plush leather office chair. The casefile for her new case was already open on the desktop, and as she watched a memo window opened, again bureau letterhead and again from Reed. It said simply, "Welcome back, Katie."

She closed her eyes and let out a long sigh. With a smile tugging at her lips, she whispered, "This is my job."

2. Eric Barnes

As Katie dug into the casefile, she found it mystifying. The victim, Eric Barnes, was only forty-two, and for the last twenty years he'd been a respected researcher in the field of Senescence. It was easy to see why, too, with his dedication. He spent ten to fifteen hours a day, six days a week, at his clinic—all of it time lost to history, because Hathor hit a brick wall half a mile from the clinic, showing nothing but a flat, gray background. A wide-angle overhead of the city showed rolling hills climbing toward the mountains, vibrant green and brown carved into blocks by the obsidian lines of the highways and shining silver roads. Right in the middle of it all, though, there was a sharp square of nothing, a 2-D gray block in the middle of 3-D reality. She'd seen that before, where the records ran thin, but nowhere in the United States for at least a decade.

She tracked down the DoD order that had made the clinic a restricted area, some nineteen years ago, but when she rolled the HaRRE display back, she found nothing helpful. Back then, coverage had been pretty spotty, anyway, and if she remembered right, Colorado was one of the last holdouts on privacy rights.

It sure seemed that way as she surveyed the state, pulling farther and farther back. There were a handful of households in Denver, flecks of color and texture on the flat background, but it wasn't until she drew back far enough to see the distant Kansas state line that she saw a real landscape. It glowed, gold and rolling to the horizon, but the rich detail stopped dead in a squiggly gray line right along Colorado's border.

That was some foresight, she thought, for the army to restrict access to one clinic within a vast plane of nothingness. She sent the record into fast forward and counted two years before the state was well and truly textured, and another fifteen months before Boulder filled in, right up to the squared border around the De Grey Clinic. Foresight, indeed.

She turned back to the case at hand, reading through the incident report. Eric Barnes had been discovered by a research assistant, Meg Ginney, three weeks ago, collapsed on his laboratory floor. At the time, he was breathing normally with some brain function, but entirely unresponsive. Katie's eyes widened as she read about his Hippocrates watch, which was exempted from the DoD restriction but never gave a word of warning. Somehow his total coma didn't trigger any alarms until just after he was found, when his blood sugar dropped too low after thirty to forty hours without eating.

His medical condition was amazing—that he could have suffered an attack sufficient to put him into a persistent coma without triggering a medical alert through Hippocrates—but the real story in Barnes's casefile grew out of conversations between the army representatives and the local police chief, who had become increasingly incautious in the last ten days. There was a conversation with Reed from two days ago, Saturday morning. She played it back out of curiosity more than anything else.

He started it off with a tired-sounding, "Hello?" She checked the timestamp, but the call had started at eleven fifteen.

"Mister Reed," a chilly woman's voice answered. "This is Police Chief Dora Hart of the Boulder City Police Department. I understand your office has been looking into the De Grey case."

"I've got an analyst on it," Reed said, noncommittal. "We haven't seen any real reason to doubt the army's medical evaluation—"

"Mister Reed, with all due respect, that report is pure fiction, and I can tell you why." The woman on the line spoke with a surprising ferocity, every word hurled into the conversation, but there was a purr in her voice that tempered it. Katie paused the audio playback and opened up HaRRE. For a moment she considered checking in on Reed, to see what had him yawning at the crack of noon, but the case was more important. She found location details on Dora Hart at the time of the call, and resumed playback with audio.

The police chief was in her office, a spacious cage in the heart of a sprawling police station, and she prowled back and forth like a lioness while she spoke with Reed. She had the army's medical report open on her desktop, and she waved to it angrily as she went on. "Barnes is a vegetable, Mr. Reed, because of his research on Gevia. I saw the scene before the army investigators came to lock the place down, and I can tell you the man was the victim of some violence."

Reed answered with a little more vigor. "I've seen stills of the man in medical care, Miss Hart—"

"Yes, *after* the army's doctors got to do their work on him." She growled and slammed a hand down on her desk. "I'm telling you, they will do anything to keep this quiet. This is a real problem for them," she said. "It's political. Gevia is important, and they don't want anyone to know what happened." Reed tried to answer, but she cut him off. "It's not *safe*, Mr. Reed. Everyone in the nation is either on Gevia or scheduled for an injection. This is too big for us to let them keep it secret. Something happened to that man, and we have to know what."

Reed didn't seem to have an answer, and finally Katie's impulse got the better of her. She shut off the playback and pulled up his medical records. She'd had her Gevia shot eight months ago, back when it was still limited to military and police forces, but she hadn't ever really thought much about it. Reed had been scheduled for a shot in December, barely a month away, but she saw he'd put it on hold after his conversation with Dora Hart. She double checked that and grinned. It had been after his conversation with Dora Hart, followed by a brief call to Brian Dimms.

She checked into the medical stills, too, to see what Reed was talking about. There was a wide shot of him on a hospital bed, naked from the waist up, pale and unconscious but otherwise looking fine. Then there were a handful of others—a close up on the back of his head showing a slight bruise beneath his thick brown hair, another one showing a bruise and abrasion on his right ring finger like someone had removed a ring forcibly, and a nick on his neck that could have happened while shaving. All of them seemed pretty inconsequential, and Reed had commented to that effect in the casefile.

She looked up at a sudden motion and saw the door to Rick's old office fly open. Reed strode out into the bullpen ahead of the GAO investigators, and Katie quickly cleared away his details from her desktop. She got rid of the medical stills, too, and pulled up Eric Barnes's personal details to track down some footage of him at home, the evening before the incident.

His location history showed him at the house at eight twenty-three, but nothing before that at all. It seemed odd, because his two-story Victorian was in a suburb west of town, well outside the clinic's restricted area. She opened up the playback at eight twenty-two, curious, and found the camera focused on the steps out front of his house. Cars rolled by on the busy residential street but there was no sign of the approaching researcher. She heard the front door open and panned the camera to find Mrs. Barnes opening the door with a warm smile, apron on, and then a moment later Eric appeared in front of her. He popped into existence on the top step, mid-stride, and Katie saw the wife give a friendly wave toward the street, but when she turned the camera back that way there was no one there.

She followed Eric into the house. He was already on the couch, feet up on a plush ottoman and reading through something on his handheld. She tried to check out what it was, but that information was restricted. In HaRRE it showed up blank. She tried switching to source video, but an error screen informed her that the video feed for this location was flagged private and reserved for household and law enforcement purposes.

That, at least, was perfectly normal. She figured half the families she knew still had their home recorders set to private. It took a simple command, run from a macro on the desktop, to request special access to the home video, but none of the cameras gave her a look at the victim's handheld screen. They were relatively low quality cameras, anyway, so she would have been very lucky to get even a guess at what he was reading. She did get a good look at his right hand, though, and she saw he was wearing a heavy gold class ring. By the time the medical examiners got to him that would be missing, but it didn't really mean much. For all she knew, they might have removed it as part of their investigation.

Theresa returned with two plates full of food, and Eric tossed aside his handheld in favor of dinner. Katie watched them eat, listened to their idle conversation about her trip to the grocery store and the book her friend had recommended. It had been years since eavesdropping like that had made Katie feel uncomfortable. It was just part of the job, now, and she zoomed in close and watched the tiny facial expressions, listened to subtle clues in the voice, watching for any indication that something was amiss. He had two hours left in the evening, before he went to bed, and he would leave in the morning before she woke up. Then he disappeared into the void, and left his mind there when he came out again.

She watched and listened, snooping for all she was worth, but there was nothing there. It seemed for all the world like a happy suburban dinner. Theresa finally heaved herself back up off the couch and held out a hand for his plate. "I could use some ice cream," she said lightly. "You want anything?"

"Maybe some coffee," he said, "if we've got any." His attention drifted to the TV, and she slipped from the room. Before she came back, a shadow fell over Katie's desk.

She looked up to meet Reed's eyes. There was something in them, sadness or pity, that took her by surprise. He said her name softly. "Katie." Before he could say more, the two investigators he'd been meeting with all morning stepped up behind him.

The one on the left fixed her with a measuring gaze and spoke firmly. "Miss Pratt," he said, spitting the words at her, "we'd like to speak with you concerning your involvement in the Buenos Aires affair."

She didn't answer right away. She didn't flinch away from his demanding gaze, either. She met it squarely, and after a heartbeat she shrugged. "I've already given a complete statement. Four complete statements, if it comes to it, and I've been interviewed on the record—"

"Miss Pratt," he cut her off, sounding bored, "we've reviewed all of your statements, but it's our job to take a full accounting. If you would just humor us, we'll try to make this quick."

She held his eyes for a moment longer, then cut her gaze to Reed. The sympathy was still there, but he shrugged. "We've got our orders, Katie. We do what they say."

She glanced down at the clock on her desktop, and just then her stomach rumbled loudly enough to make the point. She looked up again and asked without much hope, "Any chance we could do it after lunch?"

The same guy answered her with a tight smile. "This will only take a moment."

On the way across the bullpen he introduced himself, giving her a name that her headset had whispered in her ear as soon as he first approached. "Steve Fredrik, Government Accountability Office." Syllable for syllable, the same as the computerized voice. "And this is Stephen Penn, Senate Oversight. He's observing."

Katie smiled. "Watching the watcher." There was no humor in Fredrik's answering smile. "What's the focus of your investigation?"

Steve's eyes flicked to Katie, but he didn't answer her. Instead he took a long step ahead of her and led the rest of the way across the bullpen. When the door was securely shut behind him, he turned to Katie and raised an eyebrow.

"With regard to Executive Authority, this department is one of the most disorganized, haphazard, and entirely unaccountable entities in all of law enforcement. Do you understand that, Miss Pratt? Mr. Reed has been remarkably stubborn in his refusal to accept it." Reed nodded, like a dignitary graciously accepting a compliment. "But you're new here. You may not be quite so enchanted by the late Mr. Goodall's charm—"

"Charm?" Katie snapped, searching the investigator's eyes for some hint of humor. "The man tried to kill me. He was a nutcase!" Reed stiffened, and Katie rounded on him in astonishment. "Really?" she thundered. "You object to that? Are you serious?"

"Enough, Miss Pratt." Steve silenced her with a dispassionate tone. "While your objection to the late Mr. Goodall seems genuine, that in no way exonerates you from your involvement in that...fiasco in South America."

She jabbed a finger under his nose. "Watch your tone," she said. "You said you had some questions for me, and I can understand that. But I'm not going to stand here and let you accuse me. If you don't know what happened—"

The other agent, Stephen Penn, interjected smoothly, placating. "Miss Pratt," he said, "we're quite familiar with the record. Err...what there is of it."

She shook her head. "I've watched it," she said. "You have everything. He left himself out of it, but you have every shred of my involvement—"

"You'll forgive us for wanting more than your word on that." She felt fury rise up in her chest before she recognized the words. The condescending tone was clear enough. It was the same thing she'd said to Martin, accusing him of murdering his niece. Reed caught her elbow before she could hit the smug investigator, and she only struggled with him for a moment.

Reed spoke up in her defense. "I've been over this with you," he said, "and I'm not going to let you bully her. I'm acting department head here, and that makes her one of mine. You understand that?" He held Fredrik's eyes for a long moment, then nodded. "You've got your authority and we're doing everything we can to cooperate, but you're not putting one of my agents through the ringer. *Especially* after what this one's already been through."

Fredrik regarded Reed for a moment with one eyebrow raised, then spread his hands in a sign of surrender and took a long step back, ceding the floor to Stephen Penn. Penn smirked at him, then turned a smile to Katie.

"Please forgive him," he said. "He's better at audits than interviews."

His voice was smooth and his smile likable. Katie leaned back against the window with her arms crossed over her chest, chin raised. "That's an interesting game of Good Cop, Bad Cop. You boys been doing this long?"

Penn shrugged. "As my associate mentioned, this office is in a unique position with regard to oversight. It requires special effort." He handed Katie his handheld, which bore a report on her personal details. The open tab was a list of her voice communications, spanning the last month. She glanced over it and concealed a curse at what the list showed, but she figured Penn knew he had her. She scrolled idly through the list to buy a moment's time, then passed him back his handheld.

He smiled. "Anything seem odd about that to you?"

"I'm no stranger to the one-sided conversation," she said. "I like the sound of my own voice."

Fredrik spoke up from his place behind Rick's desk. "There's a pretty clear pattern there," he said. He was leaning against the wall, not sitting in the chair, but even so his position made Katie's hackles rise. The last time she'd been in here with Rick, he'd almost hit her. Fredrik leaned forward, white knuckles on the polished wood desktop, and pinned Katie with his eyes. "Why are you trying so hard to contact him? What information are you trying to pass to him?"

She looked to Reed, pleading with him to intervene again, but this time she saw only confusion in his eyes. Penn handed him the handheld, and his eyes shot wide at that. He hadn't known.

She shook her head. "It's just a stupid thing," she said. "It's nothing." Six eyes were on her now, demanding answers, and she couldn't find her voice. "It's nothing," she said again, almost stammering. "Since I was little, I like to leave messages to my dad when he can't answer the phone. It's my way of thinking. I know he won't answer, but I tell him what's on my mind, and it makes things easier."

Fredrik bit off a sharp answer. "We're not concerned about the messages to your father—"

"But it's the same thing!" She snapped at him, and knew immediately it was a mistake. The Good Cop, Bad Cop routine was working on her. She took a deep breath. "It's an old habit," she said. "I didn't really think about it. I...I've been alone. I've been trapped, first in the hospitals, and then in my apartment. You have no idea what it's like. Not after...not after what I went through. It's too much time to just sit and think." She took another deep breath and shook her head. "I have an old habit, when I need to think about something that's too close to me, and it involves making a phone call that I know won't get an answer. I just...when I was thinking about what happened in Buenos Aires, it made sense to call Martin."

Penn answered her this time. "We know what happened in your hospital room, Miss Pratt." His tone was gentle but firm. "The bureau was on to Martin's tricks by that point, and they had dumb mics recording your room." From the corner of her eye she saw Reed's cheeks flush, but she didn't begrudge him that. She was just glad he hadn't shot her at the time. "The GAO's greatest concern here is Rick's corruption. Mr. Fredrik primarily wants to discover the precise depth and breadth of your old boss's impact, but we cannot complete that investigation with any sort of certainty until we understand what led you to let one of the most powerful criminals in the world walk out of police custody."

Katie shook her head. "You think I could have stopped him?"

"I know you let him go!" Fredrik snapped, and for the first time Katie thought maybe he wasn't just playing a part. His eyes were wide, his lips peeled back in a snarl. "And you've been trying to get in touch with him like some devoted fan ever since—"

"It's not like that!" She kept her voice cool, but her breath came hot and fast. She closed her eyes, shutting out the image of his fury, and forced herself to think. Coming in today, she'd been prepared for rejection. She'd been prepared to lose her job, but she hadn't expected outright accusation. Not after so long. She'd spoken with police and federal agents, there in Buenos Aires and again at the hospital here in DC. They'd sent a representative of the court to her apartment to take a sworn deposition. It had been paperwork up until now.

She'd been trying to contact Martin, and no one had called her on that. Nobody had even mentioned it, and she'd never considered how bad it looked. Now her mind raced, trying to recall just what she'd said in all those long voicemails, but it was all vapor. She took a calming breath that didn't work, and another, and then opened her eyes to meet Fredrik's. A heartbeat had passed, maybe two. She made herself bold, and answered him with confidence, "Martin Door has done no wrong, and neither have I."

"That, my girl," he said with a sarcastic smile, shaking a finger at her, "is for us to decide."

"That's too far," Reed said, and Penn nodded his agreement.

"This has probably gotten out of hand," he said. "You have to see our side of this, though." Katie nodded once, encouraging him to go on, and he shrugged. "It looks suspicious. As you said, we have a complete record of your actions throughout the incident, but we see nothing of Martin Door. We don't hear a whisper from him, we don't see a glimpse of his face in nearly eighty hours of footage—much of it recovered from the extraordinarily secretive security system of Jesus Velez." He pronounced the name like Rick had, Jeezus Velez, right down to the good ol' boy twang, and Katie flinched. "A man who could manipulate the record like that could make you look innocent, too."

"He didn't," she said. "He can't. The system manipulates itself. It's built in. He's just not there. That's all there is to it."

Penn's expression said that would require some corroboration, and Reed jumped in to give it. "It's true. Stephen, I'm telling you, I was looking at that footage of Katie ten minutes before Rick died. There's no way he had time to fake it. I saw the condition he was in when my men arrived, and I saw with my own eyes how the cameras refused to see him. Nothing I had on me would give a double-digit identity on him, even when I pre-set it. That record is clean."

Fredrik shrugged. "It doesn't matter," he said, "because that record shows Katie busting Martin Door out of federal detention. It shows her deliberately and aggressively subverting public identity confirmation systems and cooperating in a venture that left three federal agents dead—"

"And saved the world as we know it," Reed said. "Dammit, guys, you really won't see that? If Katie hadn't gone along with Martin, none of us would be here right now. We'd be out on the streets, deputizing every police officer and security guard in the country into Ghost Targets, because Jurisprudence wouldn't be worth a damn. Velez was going to bring it down, and he was within a 'less than or equals' of doing it. Hathor would be *dead* if Katie hadn't jumped out that window."

She shot him a look of gratitude for his defense, but his eyes were locked on Fredrik's. Penn broke the staring match.

"Be that as it may," he said, "we have to do our due diligence." He tapped on his handheld and opened up a new blank recording, then said, "Now, Miss Pratt, if you would just please indulge us, tell us in your own words exactly what happened last month, beginning with your first encounter with Martin Door."

It was two more hours before she escaped Rick's old office, and when she did it was with a bang, slamming the heavy glass door behind her, with Steve Fredrik still yelling after her to take control of herself. Her head ached from the infuriating questions as much as the time she spent grinding her teeth against equally insulting responses. Her knuckles hurt from clenching her fists, and her stomach roiled from the constant wash of adrenaline and outrage. She stomped across the room, straight to the plate glass doors, and before she could give the instruction she heard Reed from back by the office saying, "Craig, open the doors for Katie." They slid open ahead of her, and Reed pounded across the room to catch up, just slipping into the elevator before the doors fell closed.

They dropped two floors before he found his voice. "I'm sorry," he said.

"You should be." She didn't look at him. Shame and anger piled up behind her eyes, and she kept her gaze locked on the doors for fear he would see them. "That was humiliating."

"That was one morning," Reed said, and she was surprised to hear chagrin in his voice. "Try going through it for three weeks."

She rounded on him. "You're kidding!"

"Hell, you were just friends with Martin for a few days. I've been a devoted assistant to Rick Goodall for nine years." He said the name like it was a curse, and she knew he was mocking the investigators.

"They can't suspect you—"

Reed cut her off with a raised hand. "They can, and they should." He smirked. "And they do." He waved vaguely toward the security recorder in the top corner of the elevator, and said, "And don't even pretend they're not listening in on us right now." He trailed off, bitter, then met Katie's eyes, "I wish I'd known about the calls to Martin."

"Reed, they were nothing—"

"I know," he said. "I believe you. But it looked bad." He sighed, and fell back against the wall of the elevator car. "But, hey, you did good. You stood up for yourself, and you survived it." He saw the doubt in her eyes and said with more sincerity, "You did good."

She snorted, and after a moment he shrugged.

"All right," he said. "But you survived it. That's what counts." He glanced at his watch and said, "Come on. Let's get some lunch."

3. Home

Paul Hafstedt from Transactions joined them at the next floor and stepped out ahead of them when they got to the lobby. Reed dragged his feet a bit until Paul got well out of earshot, then asked Katie with a suspicious nonchalance, "What sounds good for lunch?"

She glanced toward the hall that led to the cafeteria, but she suspected he wanted to get out of the building as much as she did. "Something foreign?" she said.

He grinned. "Perfect. I'm thinking Scotch." He nodded toward the big glass doors, and said, "I know just the place."

It was a cold morning, with crisp, refrozen snow along the edges of the sidewalks and a freezing fog stuffing the air like cotton. Reed said, "How cold is it?" and when a voice answered him over his headset, he shook his head. "Jesus!"

"Careful," Katie said with a stale smile. "You might get an answer."

Reed glanced over sharply, then cracked a smile of his own. "That's not funny." He glanced back over his shoulder, up and up to the mirrored windows of the Ghost Targets offices, where the Steves were probably still listening in on their conversation, and his smile slipped. "Especially not now."

"Screw 'em," Katie said. Her eyes narrowed as she caught sight of a flickering neon sign set in the wall at ankle height above a tight staircase that plunged down into darkness. She could just see a smoky window onto a room glowing with amber light, and she shook her head. "That can't be your place."

He frowned. "What's wrong with it?" He glanced back up at the office once more, then shook his head, putting the

Accountability audit from his mind. Instead he turned his full attention back to Katie and spread his hands innocently. "What?"

"Look at that place!" They were standing above it now, and a carved wood sign on the door below said simply, "Bar." The neon guttering at the top of the stairs said, "Ice cold beer." She peered down into the window and shook her head. "You can't be serious. Now, Rick...I could almost see Rick in a place like this. But not you, all buttoned-up shirt—"

"Rick brought me here," Reed said. He started to say more, but let it go. After a moment, he smiled sadly. "Come on down," he said. "Give it a chance."

The inside was exactly what she'd expected. The stale reek of real tobacco smoke hung thick in the air, and the acrid scent flooded her momentarily with memories of her father. He hadn't smoked since she was little, but the sense memory was overwhelming. Reed kept her from bumping into tables in the sudden gloom, steering her without ever quite touching her, right up to the bar.

The bartender was a big man with broad shoulders and a black ink tattoo patterning his right arm from the biceps down to the first knuckle on each finger. He had another black diamond tattoo surrounding his right eye, and even in the dim interior Katie could spot the scar that the ink was meant to hide. She didn't let her eyes linger. She gave a full turn before she took her seat, taking the place in, and when her eyes came back to the bartender, she met his gaze with one of appreciation. "Nice little place you've got here."

He laughed, a deep belly laugh that rolled around the bar until he finally wheezed to a stop. "Lady, that look on your face has been screaming for a mop and a bucket since you walked in the door." He hesitated for a moment, considering, and said, "Well, mostly. There was just a moment there—"

"I get it," she said. "You pay attention." She turned to Reed. "What's good here?"

The bartender answered for him. "This guy's gonna have three fingers of a single malt and a tall ice water. Nothing I can do to talk him into a sandwich." He jabbed a finger at her. "You should try my nachos. Or the cheese fries if you want some real fun."

"Nachos," Katie said. "And a diet coke."

Reed shook his head. "Get her a beer."

"Coke," she said more firmly, and when Reed started to object she said, "Some of us have to get back to work."

"A beer won't kill you," Reed said, while the bartender poured a generous portion of scotch in a glass at his right hand. "Besides, I don't see any reason to go back up there."

She colored. "I've...I'm sure you don't remember, but I've already walked out on the job in the middle of the day here. I can't afford to make a habit of it."

"I do remember," he said. "I'm the one who made him call you back." He rattled the ice in his glass, then took a slow sip and set it back down on the bar in front of him. His eyes were fixed on the ice. "But this is not the same thing. You're not going back up to the office because you have a plane to catch."

She frowned, and when he didn't give her any more information, she pulled out her handheld and drew up her scheduled events. Sure enough, she was booked on a flight out of town in three hours. She checked the details and said, "When did that happen?"

"Craig set it up for you while we were in your interview," Reed said. "They disabled all notification messages so we wouldn't be disturbed."

"In light of that..." she trailed off, bewildered. She tried again. "Excuse me for saying, sir, but with everything that's going on, should we really be leaving?"

He looked up from his glass and met her eyes. "They could have stopped us, Katie. They've got the authority, and they know it. I've had my ticket booked since Saturday, and they haven't done a thing to keep me here. I suspect their audit will probably go a little more smoothly with us out of the way."

She watched his eyes for a moment, but his thoughts were clearly somewhere else. He took another drink, absently, his eyes far away. Her voice sounded small in the empty bar when she said, "What have they done to you, Reed?"

It took him a moment to focus on her, and then he smiled a sad smile. "It's not them, Katie. They're just doing their job." He took a deep breath, and let it out slowly. He looked around the dim room, taking in the empty booths lost in shadow, the scratched felt of the pool table, the dart boards on the wall. "It's Rick."

"Reed, he was—"

"I know," he cut her off gently. "I know what he was, at the end, but he was my friend for a long time before that. He was my mentor, Katie. He taught me everything I know about police work." He took another deep breath, let it go, then sipped on his drink. The ice rattled against the glass in the room's silence. "I was able to get into Velez's records before his system blew. That's part of how I know...." He trailed off, but Katie knew what he'd meant to say. It was how he knew she was innocent. Martin, too. He'd seen some measure of the hell they'd gone through in Velez's lair. "I saw him gunned down, and I was what—a block away."

She caught his eyes and held them for a moment. "And it would have been me, too, if you had been any farther," she said. "Reed, you saved the day. You saved my life—"

"And I've been answering for it ever since." He finished his drink in a gulp, just before the bartender came back in through the kitchen door. Lee was carrying a big plate mounded high with chips and cheese, and as he approached the smell of it made Katie's stomach rumble again. Reed put on a smile and shook his head. "You've got the world's best timing, Lee. Pour me another."

Katie stopped him with a sharp look. "You don't need another, Reed. It's the middle of the day."

His lips tightened. "I don't fly well." He looked up at the bartender and nodded once, briefly. Before Katie could object again, he spoke over her, "Let it go, Katie. I'm your boss now, so stop trying to tell me what to do." He turned to her and quirked an eyebrow. "What can you tell me about our case?"

"It's weird," she said. She glanced over a new message on her handheld, then put it away and focused on Reed. "They've got some serious security measures in place. It'll take some time to figure out a full list of what's getting hidden—"

"We can get that," Reed said. "If they're doing everything on the books, you wouldn't believe the paperwork, but we'll be able to get a complete list. If they're doing anything under the table, our analysts will be able to track it down."

She nodded slowly, considering the implications. After a moment she said, "Okay. That helps. The whole clinic is a total blackout, but I saw him step out of thin air at his doorstep, so I knew there was something weird going on."

"Probably a private taxi," Reed said. "They do that sometimes, so people can't just watch the boundaries of a restricted area to plot comings and goings. I'm not surprised they're doing it with De Grey." He took a sip of his drink, then said, "Anything suspicious?"

"Not really," she said. She considered Reed out of the corner of her eye for a moment. "Well, just the police chief." When he didn't respond, she pressed on, "Dora Hart. She contacted you on Saturday."

"I recall," he said.

"If not for her, we wouldn't be in this. The army has done what looks like a thorough examination; the wife is content with their evaluation, but this Hart wants us to get involved."

"She had a thing with Barnes." Reed let her ponder that for a moment before he went on. "Something...what, twenty-four years ago. They went to high school together."

"That's a pretty tenuous connection."

Reed nodded. "Yeah," he said. "Yeah, it is. But she's the only agitator in this whole business, so you've got to ask yourself why. She had a relationship with the victim two decades ago, but nothing since then. I checked up on her, and even with all the gaps in his record, there's no way these two were involved recently."

"So you think she's got a good reason for agitating."

"I don't think she's got a bad one," he said. "She's a good cop. Her record attests to that. And she plays politics well; that's how she got where she is now. Fighting the army on this—and the wife—that's not good politics, so she's got to have some real conviction behind it. She's spotted something that makes her think our victim is getting the short end of the stick, and she just can't let it go." He took another drink and nodded. "I think there's a real case here."

Katie leaned back from her lunch and pulled out her handheld again. She drew up Dora Hart's personal profile and started catching up. After a while she spoke without looking up. "You got a suspect yet?"

"Three or four," he said, and gave that same tight smile again when she looked to him for more information. "That's pretty much everyone he knows. The man's a hermit."

"Well, it shouldn't take too long to track down, anyway." She checked her itinerary again, then drained the rest of her Coke with two gulps. "If we're really going to do this, I've got to get packed," she said.

"No problem." He made no move to rise. Instead, he waved goodbye with a short gesture. "I'll see you at the gate."

She hesitated, worried about leaving him there like that. She took one step away, then turned back. "Are you going to be okay?"

"I'll be fine," he said. He looked around the bar again, that same sadness still deep in his eyes. "I've just got to get out of this place."

"Fine," she said. "I'll see you at the gate."

The cold hit her as soon as she stepped outside, but a car was already waiting for her curbside. It called her name, and the door swung open as soon as she rose to street level. She climbed in and pulled the door closed behind her with a shiver. Fans hummed to life in the floorboard, flooding the car's interior with warm air, and after a moment her shivers settled.

The driver already had a course plotted to her apartment, so she blacked the windows and settled back into her seat. Eyes closed, she spoke to her headset. "Hathor, connect me to Dad." She could have used another command to record him a voice message without the wait, but there was something comforting in the ritual of it. She waited through two rings, then agreed to record a message. Her head fell back against the seat, and she let her eyes drift closed.

"Hey, Dad," she said, "It's almost three and I'm done for the day. Worse than I'd hoped, better than I'd feared." She took a deep breath, then let it go. "No," she said. "That's not quite right. I had a...an interview—" Her voice caught, and she pounded a closed fist against her leg just above the knee. "I got interrogated by Accountability," she said. "Did you ever have to answer to Internal Affairs? I don't remember you ever talking about it." She took a calming breath, and felt better when she let it go.

"I have a case," she said. "I'm working with Reed on it, actually. He's the new boss, and I'm glad. He seems like a good guy." She hesitated again, frowning, and pulled out her handheld. She left the screen blank, though, and went on after a moment. "He's still loyal to Rick."

She trailed off and for a while lost herself in the ride. Twice Hathor beeped at her, asking if she'd finished the message, and both times she told it to keep recording, but she didn't say anything else to her dad as the miles rolled by.

Finally she leaned forward, elbows on her knees, and squeezed her eyes shut. "It's going to be a weird case, Dad. I'm going to Boulder, Colorado, to figure out what happened to a famous doctor. He's in a coma." She glanced at her handheld, still blank, and put it away. "There's brain activity, but he's totally unresponsive. It's been more than a week, and the doctors don't expect him to come out of it." A flashing indicator on the driver monitor caught her eye. She was almost to her apartment. She sat back again and shook her head. "I'll try to keep you posted, but it promises to be a rough week. Love you, Dad. Goodbye."

She reached up and brushed a tear from her eye as the car pulled to a stop, then braced herself against the cold and threw the door open. The temperature had dropped six degrees since she'd left the bar, ten since they'd stepped out of the office, and the wind was howling now. She sprinted the short distance across her courtyard, pitching awkwardly as she favored her injured leg, and then had to fumble in her pockets for the key to her front door. "Open sesame," she said, as she waved the key in front of the door's sensor, then darted in and slammed the door shut behind her.

"Show me the weather forecast on the TV," she said, and her home system processed the request for her. Even as the weather radar flashed on the screen, a sinking feeling clawed at her gut and her shoulders drooped. "Oh, no," she said. "Show me the weather forecast for Boulder, too." The TV divided into split screen, and she groaned. In the mountains, it was going to be even colder. "Great," she said. "Turn that off and put on some music." Then she headed to the fridge for a drink.

She filled a glass with ice and took out a pitcher of tea. As she kicked the door shut behind her, her eyes scanned her living room. The walls were a sea foam green, now, but she was about ready to go back to the rose trim and white walls. She couldn't count the number of times she'd redone the decor in the last month. The furniture was soft, the service excellent, but this place was her prison. She felt a sudden bond with Reed, thinking back to the last thing he'd said in the bar. She needed to get out of this place.

That took her back to the dreadful interview with the investigators, and as she carried her iced tea back to the bedroom to get packed, she found herself grinding her teeth in irritation. "Hathor, connect me to Dad. No, wait. Goodbye." She broke the connection before it could even ring, and a mischievous glint sparked in her eye. "Hathor, connect me to Martin Door."

Two rings, and before the system could even prompt her she said, "Yes, voice message." She set her glass down on the dressing table in her room and moved to look out the window as a light snow began to fall. "I'm under investigation because of you," she said. She laughed. "Are you even listening to these messages? Any of them? There's no reason you should, but I'd like to think you have. I know there are others listening to them, though."

She sighed. "Government Accountability Office is after me. Reed, too. They want to know how much we had to do with the whole Velez plot. They've got my records—thank you for that— and Reed swore today that those records are legitimate, but these guys want more." She turned her back on the window and leaned against it while she looked over her room.

"I...I don't know why I'm telling you this. I'm not going to leave you any more messages. I guess that's it. It seemed weird to me to just stop calling, so I thought I should explain, but...." She trailed off, her gaze sinking to the floor, and then shook her head.

"You're not helping yourself," she said. "I wish you hadn't run. It's not the first time I've said that, but it's still true. We could use what you know, and I'm sure I could have protected you...." The words tasted like a lie, and the memory of Fredrik's hateful visage suddenly boiled up behind her eyes. "They think you're a monster," she said. "What are you up to?"

It wasn't the first time she'd asked him that question, but there was never any answer. He was the most capable ghost left in the world, the last of Hathor's creators, roaming free and carrying with him all the work of the madman that had nearly brought the whole system down barely a month ago. He had become a friend, in just a few short days, and then disappeared completely.

Her mind jittered, dancing across the things she'd said to him, the things she wanted to say. She thought about her interview and frowned. A moment later she said, "I don't know if you remember, but you once told me you would do what you could to clear my name." That memory of Fredrik came back again, leaning on his white knuckles, face twisted in rage. "That's...that's not what I'm calling about. Okay? Reed is on my side here, and I've given the absolute truth in every statement they've asked for. The stuff you've provided, they say they can't trust it, anyway. So that's not what I'm calling about."

She could remember him with kind, fatherly eyes, promising to protect her. She could remember him looking like a child, helpless, thanking her for giving him hope. Mostly she remembered him leaving, bruised and bloodied, but with a swagger born of a new determination. That was the man she didn't know. She had a pretty good grasp on the other shades of Martin Door, but the one who'd walked away with Velez's secrets in the palm of his hand, that one was a mystery to her.

"I hope you're all right," she said. She shook her head and said, "Goodbye."

After that she didn't much feel like talking. The music playing over the room's speakers matched her mood, muted and sad, and after a moment she threw the curtains wide again so she could watch the snow drift down while she packed. Craig's itinerary had her away for a week, but her favorite bag wouldn't hold much more than four days' worth of clothes. She decided to risk it. She could do some shopping in Boulder if it came to it. She packed warmly, with an eye to comfort more than anything else. Reed always wore the button-down suit, she thought, so let him carry the attention. She worked better in jeans, anyway. Somehow, she didn't think her boss would complain.

Half an hour to get packed and another hour killed on her handheld just passing the time, then she called for a car and made a mad dash across the courtyard as it pulled up. There was a quarter inch of snow on the ground, enough to show her footprints clearly against the mat of dead grass, and according to the reports there'd be a full inch on the ground before nightfall.

Not her problem, though. Last she'd seen, there were eighteen inches on the mountain outside Boulder, and two of the interstates out of town were closed down. But the airport was reporting no delays, and her handheld showed her Reed was on his way to the gate already. She sighed as she closed the door and told her driver unnecessarily, "Take me to the airport. Make it quick." Then she snuggled into the chair and slipped into a doze while the car maneuvered into traffic. Outside, the snow fell.

4. At De Grey

Reed was already seated on the plane when Katie got to the airport, and her headset started buzzing warnings to her while she was running to the gate. She pulled out her handheld without breaking pace and confirmed her seat. An attendant closed the boarding doors behind her, and while Katie was still settling into her chair, the plane headed for the runway.

She wasn't sitting next to Reed, which was almost a relief. She could see him from her place, one row up and six seats over, his head resting on the window glass and his eyes staring unseeing out into the snow. He was a mess. She wondered in passing how much trouble he was going to be, working this case.

In the end it didn't matter much, she decided as the jet's lunge into the sky pressed her back into her seat. If it came down to it, she could handle the case. This was nothing like the Linson murder, with malicious ghosters threatening to obscure the whole database. It was a passive gap in the archive, arranged within the bounds of law, and she had every reason to believe it could be sorted out with a little pressure in the right places. Maybe the local police chief didn't have the necessary authority to get things done, but a couple FBI agents from Ghost Targets should be able to open doors.

With that little pep talk at the front of her mind, she turned to the case, pulling out her handheld as the plane settled in at cruising altitude. She went back to Dora Hart, double-checking Reed's facts, and came to the same conclusion. The police chief and the victim had had more than a passing friendship in high school, but they'd lost touch for nearly a decade after that and hadn't exchanged more than occasional notes in the time since then—Christmas cards and catch-ups, and the occasional suggestion that they get together for dinner sometime, but she could find no record of them following through on that.

She peeked into Barnes's research, wondering what she might find there, but there wasn't much of it to see. All of his recent work had been done under strict confidentiality, and many of his old papers had been confiscated and restricted when he first went to work at De Grey. She had to go back to his undergraduate work to find anything more than an abstract, and when she did that she realized access to his newer papers wouldn't have done her any good. It was all way over her head.

Right as she was closing out a paper on epigenetics he'd written for his Freshman biology class, the plane began its final descent. She caught a glimpse of the snowy mountainside out the window when she threw a glance at Reed, forehead still resting on the window, but his body slumped forward at an uncomfortable angle. She pocketed her handheld and said quietly into her headset, "Hathor, connect me to Reed."

He jerked awake on the first ring and answered her on the second as he craned an obviously stiff neck to pick her out on the row behind him. "What?"

"I thought you might want a moment to pull yourself together," she said. "Chief Hart is meeting us at the airport."

She saw him frown, brows knitting together. "She is?"

"Got a message mid-flight. She got us clearance to visit the clinic tonight, which is apparently something of a feat." She watched him run a hand through his hair, eyes bloodshot and a little panicky, and her heart went out to him. "Miles to go before we sleep, sir."

"Thanks, Katie." He nodded to her, then settled back into his chair, running his hand through his hair again. "Goodbye."

By the time they reached the terminal, he looked better, and when they stepped out into the winter chill, he seemed himself. His shoulders were square, his suit hung easily on a powerful frame, and his emerald eyes captured those of Dora Hart, waiting for them by her black-and-white cruiser. She wasn't tall—maybe an inch taller than Katie—but the woman wore strength like a tailored suit. Her uniform jacket hung open over a tight-fitting white T-shirt that showed off her muscle tone. She flashed a confident smile when she saw Reed looking her way.

She called to him, "You my man?"

He nodded back, and smiled as he stepped up and extended a hand. "I'm Special Agent Reed, FBI."

"Of course you are," she purred, then cast a fleeting glance on Katie. "And this is?"

Katie nodded back at her. "Katie Pratt, also of Ghost Targets."

"Well," Hart said, her full attention back on Reed's eyes. "I'm glad you could make the time to visit Boulder. I'm sure we won't disappoint." She glanced at Katie again, and her mouth turned down. "Oh, you poor thing," she said. "Let's get in the car. You look miserable."

Katie's lips tightened, but neither of the others noticed. All three climbed into the car, and as soon as the doors were closed Hart said, "Dispatch, send us to the De Grey Clinic, private entrance. Thanks." The cruiser was a six-seater, two benches facing each other, and Chief Hart settled in facing Reed, sitting in the center of her bench with both arms up on the seat back. "I do apologize for the abrupt change of plans, but we got lucky finding an opportunity at all. I understand the assistant is resuming Eric's research at eight tomorrow morning, and it would be a real bitch to try to get in once they're operational again."

"The assistant," Katie said, trying to cue Reed in. "That would be Meg Ginney? She's been with the De Grey clinic for four years now."

"Yes, dear." Hart threw her a condescending look for stating the obvious. "You've done your research, I see."

Reed missed the exchange. He leaned forward, elbows on his knees, and said, "What do we know about his condition?"

The police chief looked away, some of her bravado suddenly gone, and shrugged one shoulder. "He's comatose, unresponsive. Doctors say there's nothing they can do for him. His wife has him on machines."

Katie spoke up. "There are signs of normal brain activity," she said, and got a withering look for it. She tilted her head, confused at the reaction, and said defensively, "He's been out long enough that his odds aren't good, but he's not exactly a vegetable."

Reed shook his head. "Sounds complicated. What makes you think there was a crime involved?"

The chief hesitated for a moment, her breath caught in her chest, then let it all out in a *whuff.* "It's the cover-up," she said. "I don't have anything to go on but that. But they're hiding something, and that much is plain as day."

Reed tried to sound diplomatic. "Chief Hart, I can't force an investigation within a military restricted area based on your hunch—"

"You don't have to," she said, pulling her chin up and meeting his eyes. "That's what this is for. That's exactly why we're going there now, so you can see for yourself. And you will see. Something strange is going on at that lab."

"Yes," Katie said, a little more bitterly than she intended. "They're putting the last nail in the coffin of aging. That's a miraculous thing."

"And every man, woman, and child in the country is waiting with bated breath for their chance to take the drug," Hart said, rounding on her. "They check their handhelds every morning for any news at all about it, and you know what they haven't seen? They haven't seen that the lead researcher is comatose in his own lab. They haven't read a word about his inexplicable, bizarre accident or the medical implications of it. Neither has anyone in the medical community. The army has this story under lockdown, Miss Pratt, and there's something very wrong about that."

"I agree," Reed said, reaching out a hand to soothe her. "We'll do everything we can. Our office has considerable pull, even where we lack direct authority. That's why we're here."

"Thank you," Hart said, grateful eyes wide as she met Reed's. "Thank you so much. I just need to know that I've done everything I can."

In spite of that last, she remained in the car when they arrived at the clinic. "I'm heading back to the precinct to take care of some paperwork," she said to Reed. "Just give me a buzz when you're done here, and I'll be right by to drop you at your hotel."

He reached for the door handle, but she stopped him with a light finger on his other wrist. "Do call me. We'll need to talk before you call it a night."

He nodded his understanding with a polite smile and then left the car. Katie was already waiting outside the other door, and she rolled her eyes as the car backed out and disappeared through the security gate and back into traffic. "Can you believe that woman?"

"What?" Reed said. "Katie, she's grieving. Cut her some slack."

Katie stared for a moment, then shook her head. Before she could say more, a voice interrupted on her headset, and by his reaction Reed was hearing the same thing. "You are loitering in a restricted area. Please proceed directly to the administrative building and check in with the receptionist there. All monitoring devices are disabled in this area including Hathor-enabled headsets and handhelds, Hippocrates devices, and any remote personal assistant connections. You are loitering in a restricted area. Please proceed—" Katie silenced her headset with a flick of her wrist, and after a moment's thought pulled it off her ear and dropped it into her pocket, next to the handheld displaying a connection status error.

"Hadn't considered that," she grumbled to Reed. "Which one's the administrative building?"

"That one," Reed said, pointing to the largest of the clinic's four bone-white buildings. "But the girl in the research lab is expecting us, so we can go on there." He fell into a trot toward the nearest of the buildings, to their left.

Night was setting in, violet in the sky, but the grounds of the clinic glowed eerie white beneath a phalanx of streetlights. There wasn't a shadow, and she noticed with a sickening recognition the security cameras mounted on all the light poles. They weren't weapons—as far as she knew, no one in the world used the security system that nutcase Velez had invented for himself—but the cameras were the same model. She felt their electronic eyes passing over her and remembered that room. She shivered, and it had nothing to do with the cold.

Reed seemed to notice. He walked a little closer to her, and picked up his pace toward the lab.

The rough sandstone building was a squat square, sprawling thousands of square feet but mostly just one floor. The center of the building rose up to a second floor, putting Katie in mind of a squared-off top hat. The entrance was a single glass door, tinted almost black, set at an angle in the southeast corner of the building under a small overhang. Katie glanced up above the door where she'd have expected another camera to monitor their approach, but the wall was empty. She turned in surprise, and realized with a sense of dread that none of the cameras on the grounds ever turned this way. Reed seemed to grasp what she was thinking, because he only turned down a corner of his mouth and shrugged.

"It's never easy."

The door flew open as they approached, pushing the grim thought from her mind. A young woman met them on the threshold, with a deeply concerned look in her eyes. "Goodness!"

she said, reaching out an arm toward Katie. "It's a nasty night out there! Come into the warmth."

The girl was in her twenties, wearing jeans and a cute yellow blouse, and a thin silver chain around her neck. She extended a delicate hand to Katie and said, "I'm Meg. Research assistant here."

Katie shook the offered hand and made introductions while she took in the building's lobby. Meg had short red hair, somewhere between curly and frizzy, and kind green eyes. The room they were in was a small foyer, with a receptionist stand directly opposite the entrance and a door into an empty guard booth just beyond it. Tinted windows gave a smoky view on the iridescent snowfall outside, and low-backed, minimalist couches stood along the interior walls on either side. The whole lobby was barely wider than a corridor, a big right angle with heavy steel security doors set into the interior wall at each end, and nothing else.

Katie nodded toward one of the doors. "I guess the lab is in there?"

Meg looked over her shoulder and then back to Katie with a nod. "Yes," she said. "Oh, right down to business. Good." There was a vacancy in her response that had nothing to do with mental acumen. She was grieving, too. Katie couldn't help thinking what a sad lot they all were.

Meg approached the door and opened it with a set of three small steel keys on a ring. Reed whistled low. "You've got to be kidding."

Meg looked over her other shoulder at him and shook her head with deep gravity. "There is nowhere in the world more important to human survival than this facility, Mr. Reed." She released the last of the locks and heaved the door open for them. "I understand you're here to help Eric, and he is a dear friend of mine, but you'd better come here with a real reverence for the secrecy of what we do."

Reed nodded briefly and slipped past her into the medical lab. Katie went more slowly and held Meg's eyes instead of checking out the room. "That's...that's got to be something of an overstatement, Miss Ginney."

The research assistant shook her head furiously. "Gevia represents the end to human aging. It's...they're still billing it as experimental, but it works. It *works*, and it's *safe*, and we know enough now to get it to everyone." She blinked, suddenly hesitant, and shrugged her shoulders. "Everyone in America, anyway."

Katie made a mental note of the girl's resentment, but changed tacks. "How much of a setback is it losing Barnes, though? It's my understanding that he's the brains behind Gevia—"

"Oh, he is," Meg nodded, eyes wide, "but we'll carry on. You have no idea how much he's done, how much he's accomplished, with his work. We can't let that go away, Miss Pratt. We can never allow that to happen." As she trailed off, her eyes drifted down the length of the huge, open lab to a far corner. The lights were dimmer there, and thin hospital curtains concealed the whole corner of the room. The shadows there danced with the electric green flicker of monitoring equipment, and Katie heard or imagined the soft hiss and whine, the idle beeps tracking a weak pulse behind the curtains. Some of the color fled from her face.

"He's here?"

Meg must have heard the horror in her voice, because her eyes snapped to Katie's with a burning intensity. "It's the only place he's *safe*," she said. "He's famous. You probably can't understand, but when I studied him in medical school they talked of him like a god. The man unraveled the secrets of death, Miss Pratt. Nothing in medical science rivals that. Not refrigeration, not penicillin, not even the cancer vaccine."

Katie frowned. "I thought he worked on the cancer vaccine."

"He did," Meg said. "And even that doesn't compare to what he's doing here." She took a deep breath, worshipful, and then squared her shoulders and turned toward the corner that kept drawing her eyes. "Come with me," she said. "I'll introduce you."

They headed across the pristine tiled floor. Everything was white—the floor, the ceiling, the massive filing cabinets that lined all four walls, broken only by the two doors out into the lobby and another two opposite, that probably led to a bathroom, maybe a storage closet. The floor of the lab was broken regularly by islands, tall lab tables eight feet long and four feet across, each of them bisected by a long row of connections for the myriad heaters and burners and meters and miscellaneous research apparatus stored in the cabinets beneath. Katie thought back to the chemistry lab she'd used in high school class, and she could recognize the setup, but this was far more sophisticated.

The tabletops were clearly interactive desktops, and the ghostly holographic projection of a white rat hovering over the second desk to her left suggested they might all be 3-D desktops. She couldn't fathom the expense of setting up this many stations with that level of technology, especially for a staff of, apparently, two.

As soon as that thought crossed her mind, she asked the question. "You said you're the research assistant here. How many researchers work in this facility?"

"In *this* facility?" Meg tossed Katie a look of incredulity. "One. Two. Uhh...look, we're the only ones allowed in here. It's just Eric and me." She frowned. "And Cohn."

"Cohn is a scientist?"

Meg snorted. "Hardly. Ellie Cohn is our military liaison. The army put her here. She's got full access to Eric, and she's *always* here. All she does is interfere."

Katie watched Meg out of the corner of her eye. "Does the military involvement corrupt Eric's research?"

"No," she shook her head slowly. "Umm...no. No. He's too careful for that. You can compensate for external factors—" She took a deep breath. "Sorry. No, they just make everything complicated. They get in the way. Gevia..." she trailed off, her eyes on her hands, then suddenly met Katie's gaze with eyes begging for understanding. "Gevia shouldn't be a national resource, Miss Pratt. The army shouldn't be involved at all. We should have dispensaries set up in every cul-de-sac and dirty little village across the world." She sighed. "Eric could've done that. He was working on logistics for it for a while, but Ellie put a stop to that."

She stopped in front of the curtain and took another deep breath. She looked over at Katie. "They've got their own plans, Miss Pratt, that have nothing to do with medicine. I don't trust them." She reached up, eerily slowly, and then flipped the curtains back with an almost casual gesture. "He trusted them, though."

Eric Barnes looked peaceful. He lay at rest on a narrow but luxurious bed, nothing like the mechanical monsters still in use in Argentina hospitals, Katie thought. Her lips twisted into a sardonic grimace. There weren't any of the garish monitors she'd imagined, either, but a single computer monitor suspended on the wall above him with readouts for each of dozens of monitors on him. His IV fed from a pressurized supply hidden somewhere in the bed, and there was no sign of breathing machinery. She recognized the electrodes hooked up to his arms and legs, intended to stimulate muscle action, and she shook her head.

"How much does this cost?"

"It doesn't matter," Meg said, and her tone brooked no further discussion. The sheets on his bed bunched around his waist, revealing a trim upper torso, surprisingly fit for someone in an office job. He was strikingly handsome, distinguished, and the whole setup gave the appearance of a man who'd just dozed off while reading. A plush armchair stood nearby, with a bedstand,

and Katie got the feeling he had pretty regular company. She glanced at Meg and saw her eyes fixed on Eric's face.

It was a good face, still and serene, high cheekbones and good thick brown hair—almost black. She knew that couldn't last, no matter how expensive the setup. He would wither. His cheeks would sink, his strong arms would shrivel down to twigs. He would lose his color, and eventually he would lose his hair. Medical science had come a long way in the years of Barnes's research, but they still couldn't fake humanity in a piece of warm meat. She knew that all too well.

She had to fight down an angry emptiness at the thought, at the images that swam up with it, and she turned on her heel and darted away just as a surprised Reed stepped up past her. She heard him take over the interview, asking Meg probing questions about Eric's contacts, his most recent projects, and the political pressure he was under. Katie couldn't linger long enough to learn the answers. She almost stumbled in her haste and caught herself on the edge of one of the lab tables. Trying to think of anything but the man behind the curtain, she examined the table, but it was covered in notes that meant nothing to her.

She moved to the next table, where Reed had somehow activated the controls for the holograph projector. There, three human models hung suspended in the air above it. One was clearly a muscle-mass frame, with skin and bone stripped away, and another showed only organs, and the third...she considered it for some time before guessing it was a graphic representation of an immune system, but she couldn't be sure of that. She looked for some notes on the table's surface, but again it was incomprehensible to her.

Katie turned away, and her eyes fell on the long rows of cabinets along the wall. Her head tilted as curiosity took over, and she approached the white steel doors with a look of interest. Something in her expression must have concerned the young research assistant, because she rushed across the room to intercept Katie. The girl was three steps too slow.

"What's this?" Katie asked, pulling open the nearest cabinet door.

"It's nothing," Meg said, a touch breathless. She reached out to push the door closed, but Katie held it open with one rigid finger. She bent forward to look more closely, even as Meg repeated herself. "It's nothing!"

The cabinet she'd picked had five shelves filled with identical black leather-bound books. Their spines were empty of any titles or other identifying text, but they showed varying ages and use, a progression of decay from left to right, top to bottom. The spines of the books on the top shelf were cracked and worn, almost gray with use. The whole set looked more expensive than any lab notebooks Katie had ever seen, but everything about this clinic astonished her.

She reached for a random book on the shelf, but Meg physically intervened, squeezing awkwardly into the narrow gap between Katie and the books. "What are you doing? These have nothing to do with—"

"What are they?" Katie asked. She took a step back, which clearly put the girl more at ease. Meg glanced toward the researcher's resting place, then visibly relented.

She knelt, sinking down on her heels, and plucked a book off the second shelf from the bottom. She flipped open the heavy cover and passed it to Katie, who found a scrawled, barely legible script on the slightly yellowed, lined pages. Halfway down the first page in an oversized curl, she read a title. "*Teleos*, a novel by Eric Barnes." Three lines farther down, the novel started with a cramped ten-line paragraph that was entirely marked out. Meg glanced over the top of the book and blushed.

"Oh," she said. "He, uh...he scrapped the prologue." She flipped forward six or seven pages, and Katie saw every line on each of those pages neatly scratched out with a single line of black ink. Meg turned to a page labeled "Chapter One" and said, "Start there."

Katie started into the first page, and lost herself more in the process of puzzling out his handwriting than in the actual storyline. She couldn't remember the last time she'd seen a full page of handwriting. It brought back memories from grade school and even earlier. She remembered her dad teaching her how to scratch her name onto a magnetic drawing board when she was tiny. She'd written him a letter from the Academy, an actual letter on paper, and he had cried when he read it, according to her mom. He'd always called it a lost art.

She snapped from her memories with a start, and her eyes flashed to the cabinet packed full of these writing books. She counted forty books on the top shelf, which put two hundred in this one cabinet, and by the looks of it he'd filled at least a hundred, hundred and twenty of them. Her eyes grew wide. "Are these all...." She trailed off, then took a step back and looked down the long row of cabinets, dozens of them, and her jaw dropped. "Are these all full of—"

"Hah! What?" Meg's face split in a smile. "No. No." She took the book from Katie's numb fingers and snapped it smartly shut, then put it away and closed the cabinet. She caught Katie's eye before she opened the next cabinet over to the right. It held shelves full of more scientific equipment. Meg gave a flourish, and shook her head, still smiling. "I thought you were some kind of super sleuth, picking that one cabinet—"

"Still," Katie said. "He writes? By *hand*?"

Meg shrugged. "Our recordings aren't always reliable. With all the money that goes into our equipment, they spend ten times as much keeping this place secret, and that costs us reliability. Eric just got in the habit of putting stuff on paper, and we've all sort of picked it up over the years."

That struck Katie as useful information, and the trained cop tucked it away for later consideration, but her curiosity was getting the better of her. "But he's a *writer*?" Katie's head tilted again, and her nose scrunched as she leaned in close and whispered, "Is he any good?"

Meg shrugged one shoulder. "He's a lot better now than when he started. But that's not the point. It was never about writing books. It's just something he does to help him think. When his research has him stumped, he'll leave it open wherever he's working, wander over here and grab his current book, then sit down at that table there and just spend some time scribbling." She leaned back against the closed cabinet doors, and her eyes were on something far away.

"The first time I saw him do it," she said with a slight shake of her head, "I was furious. I was new here. I just got thrown in while he was in the middle of a major project trying to figure out why Gevia worked better in theater than it does on leave, and some people were saying that had implications that could doom the whole project, and he put me through a crash course on operating the tables just so I could pull up fifteen different simulations for him, and then he stood and watched them run. Over, and over, and over, without explaining to me at all what was going on. Then he looked at me, held my eyes for a long moment, and said, 'I've got it. Jeri and Dianne are sisters.' And he came over here, pulled out a book." Her smile widened. "And wrote the next-to-last chapter of *Georgia Falls*, which is still my favorite." She trailed off, but Katie let her have the memory. When she came back around, she shook her head a little and then pushed her eyes up to Katie's.

"Then he snapped the book closed, and said, 'Of course.' He made the tiniest adjustment to half of the simulations, and *bam*, there was our deviation. He decided one of the inoculations they were getting on deployment was interfering positively with the Gevia effect, and six months later we had the chemical combination synthesized, refined, and integrated into our core formula." She sighed. "And Jeri married Troy beneath the Georgia moon. It was perfect."

Her eyes drifted back to Barnes's place in the corner, as Katie had known they would, and the girl's smile faded. "He's spent more time in this room than outside it for thirteen years now, Miss Pratt. It takes a special kind of man...."

Katie put a comforting hand on her shoulder. "It does," she said. "He was."

"He is," Meg corrected her firmly.

"He is." Katie looked away and made eye contact with Reed. He asked a question with his eyes, and Katie answered it with a quick nod.

He crossed the room to join them. "I think we've got everything we need, Miss Ginney. Thank you for your time."

"Of course," she said, dashing a hand at her eyes. She took a ragged breath. "Is there, umm...if there's anything I can do for you..."

"We'll be in touch," Katie said, and offered her a comforting smile. "Thank you."

Meg walked them to the door. She stood there, silhouetted in the clinic's sterile white light, while Katie and Reed made their way out onto the chilly grounds.

5. Mrs. Barnes

Katie and Reed walked in silence, lost in their own thoughts, until they passed through the outer gates. Immediately their headsets went off, emitting a loud twin buzzing that startled them both. Reed reacted first, fishing the revived headset from his pocket and hooking it on his ear even as he started speaking. "Hathor, connect me to Chief Hart. Thanks."

Katie pulled out her handheld and checked the time—quarter to midnight—and tried to catch Reed's attention with a wave of her hand, but the police chief was already on the line. "Chief Hart! Hi. We're done at De Grey. Is your offer for a ride still good?" He chuckled at her answer and said, "Sure. Meet you there. Goodbye." When he finally looked at Katie, he caught her disappointed expression. "What?"

"Couldn't we have put that off to tomorrow?" She shivered and rubbed her arms briskly against the cold. "I just want to get under some thick blankets and get some rest."

He smiled ruefully. "Sorry, Katie. No rest for the weary." He turned her north and pointed to a cafe half a mile down, dim glow within the deep night. "She's meeting us there. Come on."

The walk warmed her some, but it did nothing for her attitude. She checked her handheld more than once, plotting a course from the police station to their position, and it was easily a fifteen-minute drive. "You should have called her before we left," she grumbled.

"Couldn't," Reed said. "That place is locked down tight."

"It's weird." Katie glanced through the steel bars of the fence on her left, into the eerie silver sparkle of the clinic's grounds. It seemed far away, though she could have reached out and touched the fence. "Hard to believe stepping through a gate can cut you off so completely."

He threw a glance at her that she probably wasn't meant to catch, but it was inspired by the same thought that crossed her mind. Velez's lair. She shook her head. "That was different, though. That was an underground bunker cut off from the world. This is a research lab in plain sight." She waved toward the yard they were trudging past. "It's famous. How can it be so isolated."

"It was, though." His voice was grim, and she nodded.

"I felt it," she said. "Inside there...I can only imagine what it must have been like for him."

Reed was looking back over his shoulder as they walked, his eyes on the strange building, and he nodded toward it. "Did you get a look upstairs? That was some fancy equipment."

Katie frowned and shook her head. "More lab tables?"

He laughed. "No, he had a running track. Probably how he kept in such great shape. Dynamic relational floor tiles, and WorldWindows on both sides, so he could recreate any jogging path in the world. Unless I miss my guess, he had Yellowstone on up there, and I found a pad where he'd scribbled down the codes for the Redwood Forests and the Champs-Élysées." He trailed off. "I wonder if they do people." After a moment he shook his head. "Do you have any idea what a setup like that costs?"

"It kept him in his cage," Katie said. "Have you looked over his location history? The man practically lives here. He looked happy enough with his wife, the few minutes I got to see of his home life, but he gets up before the sun and rushes in to work on his research, then he pops into existence on his front doorstep after dark." She bit her lower lip, her forehead creasing at a memory. "The assistant said they would spend ungodly amounts of money to keep their secret safe. I suppose a jogging track that keeps him in their purview would probably fit into that."

"That tells us this guy knows his way around a negotiation, then. I don't care how outlandish the budget is, it takes a savvy guy to get personal amenities out of a government administrator."

"It tells us more than that," she said. "It tells us he wasn't expecting to take a fall. And neither were his handlers, or they wouldn't have approved it."

Reed frowned. "Katie, I don't know how much you looked at his monitors—"

"Not much at all," she said, hoping he hadn't noticed how quickly she'd fled.

"Well I got a good look, while you and the girl were holding your little book club, and I dug up his medical chart, too." He sucked in a cold breath through his teeth. "Everything I see makes it look like an accident. A tragedy, sure, but I don't see anything to make me suspicious."

"Is that why you wanted to meet with the chief tonight?" Katie said, her hopes rising. "You ready to hand this back to her?"

He walked a few steps in silence, his eyes on the path beneath his feet. Then he shook his head. "I don't know about that." He forced a weak smile. "I'm not in any hurry to get back to DC." A chuckle to match the smile, and then he sighed. "I don't see the chief letting go, anyway. And, truth be told, I want to know what the hell is going on here." He stopped and turned on his heel to look back toward the clinic one more time. He put his hands up on the bars and peered through the distance. "It may not be criminal, but something strange is going on here."

"It's the secrets," Katie said. She could feel it, a deep disquiet at the power of the place. "But how much are they going to let us see?"

Reed didn't answer for a long time. But when he finally tore his gaze from the clinic, Katie's question seemed to hit him all at once. His mouth curled up in a wicked grin that climbed into his eyes. "Sometimes I forget you're new to this," he said. He waggled a finger at her, then fell back into his easy pace toward the late-night cafe. "You're a good cop, Katie, and that makes me forget how much you don't know." He chuckled. "But this is what we do. It's not a question of how much they'll let us see, but what tools we will use to peek around their blindfolds."

He fell silent for a moment, thinking. Then he started nodding, and said, "Yeah. Yeah, that's a good point. I need to get you up to speed, and this is a perfect training ground. We're seeing this one through, Katie, if only for the practice."

"I can live with that," she said, some of his enthusiasm finally reviving her spirits. Just then the black-and-white police car pulled around the corner up ahead, and flashed its brights at them twice. She sighed. "If I can get through tonight, anyway."

He laughed and clapped her on the back, then pulled the door open for her. "You'll be fine," he said. "Thanks for the ride, Chief!"

As soon as Katie ducked into the car, she regretted some of her honesty. Something in the chief's eyes told Katie she'd been listening in. By the time Reed settled beside her, though, the look was gone, replaced with an enthusiastic curiosity. She put a hand on his knee and said, "What did you find?"

"Not a lot," he said, shaking his head. "I spent half my time in there trying to find a gap where I could get a Hathor connection on my handheld." Katie's eyes grew wide. She hadn't even thought to try. Reed went on, "But there was nothing. They have that facility locked down, and they know what they're doing. Now, as far as Barnes goes—"

"I know," Hart said. "I heard." She turned her gaze out the window to the dark night. Katie saw her hands clench in fists. "There's something here, Agent Reed. Barnes had a perfect medical history. I don't know if you've had a chance to look at it in Hippocrates, but it's not just that this was unexpected. They checked. As important as he was to this program, they checked him for damn near everything. And he was clean." She shook her head. "Maybe you didn't see it. They pulled access to those tests once I started pushing for a more thorough investigation."

"Of what?" Katie said, and her voice carried more of a bark than she'd intended. She tried to soften it. "I still don't understand what you want to investigate. The man's in a coma, with no sign of violence—"

"That can be faked."

"How?" Katie snapped.

"Drugs," Hart said, snapping right back. "I guess you didn't bother to look too close, but I saw what could easily have been an injection mark on his neck."

"And that could just as easily have been part of the medical response to his condition," Katie said. "Maybe the doctors did that. Besides, if he was poisoned, wouldn't it have shown up in Hippocrates?"

"That depends. Whatever happened to him, it should have shown up in Hippocrates and it didn't. That's almost reason enough to believe it was engineered."

"Engineered? How? I don't think you can't just invent a miracle poison—"

"No?" Hart said, and she jabbed a thumb back in the direction of the clinic. "What do you think they do in there, all day, every day? What do you think those extraordinarily expensive tables are for? All you'd have to do is program a simulation on any of these tables, feed in your desired effects—a coma, say—and some key medical information about your patient—"

Katie fell back, deflated. "And they have every last detail of his medical information."

"Exactly," Hart said. "How hard would it be to make something up that would leave him like...like that?" For the first time since Katie had met her, the other woman looked weak. The chief turned away to dab at her eyes, and Katie dropped her gaze.

After a moment, Hart went on. "That's why I want an investigation. They've got the means. I just want to know what happened."

"But why would they block it?" Reed asked. "I understand they want to protect their secrets, but like you said, this guy was important to their project. Why would the army get in the way if there were anything suspicious?"

"Ellie Cohn." She spit out the name like a curse. "She was the military liaison working with Barnes, and something in my gut tells me she's up to no good. If she wanted to stop an investigation, I imagine she'd have the pull to make it happen."

"But what about the wife?" Katie said, leaning forward. "If Barnes's wife started pushing for an investigation, the army would be hard pressed—"

Hart cut her off with a bitter laugh. "The wife," she said dismissively. "That woman is worse than the army. She's done with him, Miss Pratt. You can see it in her eyes when you talk to her. He's been unconscious for a couple weeks, and she's already walked away and started her life without him." She looked back to Reed, and her eyes were pleading. "There has to be some other angle."

Reed thought about it for a while, then shook his head. "No," he said. "No, I'm pretty sure those are our two angles. But we may be able to bring a bit more strength to bear on them than you were." He looked over at Katie, considering, and said, "You've never been military, huh?"

"Cop all my life, sir."

He smiled at that. "I'll take Cohn, then. Can you handle the wife?"

Katie had to fight down a contemptuous snort. She could handle the wife. Better than this police chief, she was sure of it. All she said was, "Yeah, I'll take a run at it."

Reed nodded. "Good. Good. In the morning, of course. In the meantime, Chief Hart, I'd like to get a look at your records on the investigation so far."

A delighted smile took Hart's face, even as the car slowed to a stop. "Of course, Agent Reed. Everything I have is yours." She pushed open the door and waved to the hotel entrance just outside. "Since we're already here, though, Miss Pratt can go ahead and get some sleep, if she wants." She turned that same dark gaze back on Katie again, and said too sweetly, "You look tired, dear."

Katie smiled back, her own tight, and shook her head. "I'll be fine," she said. "Let's go to the station."

Reed clapped her on the shoulder. "I like to see that enthusiasm," he said, "but you do look tired. And I'm not convinced you're completely recovered from your incident in Argentina. Go on up and get some sleep. I'll fill you in on the details tomorrow morning."

She wanted to argue—she hated the thought of being dismissed by that woman—but she *was* tired, and not too enthusiastic about spending the rest of the night in close quarters with the chief. After a moment's tortured hesitation, she finally nodded her thanks to Reed and climbed out of the car. An instant later it sped away. She watched it go, then turned and headed into the hotel while her handheld checked her in and her headset told her the room number.

Her headset woke her the next morning with the angry trill of an alarm. She answered it with her face still stuffed in the pillow. "I'm up! I'm up!" Then a moment later, "Ten more minutes." When it went off again, she threw the covers off her and sat up, hooking the headset over her ear.

"Fine," she said, blinking bleary eyes. She grabbed her headset to check the time, 7:11 a.m., and found a voice message indicator. She sighed as she opened the message center on her handheld.

"Play me Reed's message. Thanks." She left it on, her boss talking quietly into her ear, while she got ready for the day.

She was in the middle of brushing her teeth when it occurred to her to wonder, and she grabbed the handheld from its place on the counter. The message had come in at 5:04 a.m. It was twelve minutes long, probably the whole time he'd spent in the cab between the police station and the hotel. Reed had pulled an all-nighter. She shook her head while he filled her in on the complexities of the army's involvement.

The investigation, as it stood, was currently in the wife's hands. While the army had a significant role in the clinic's operation, they couldn't release Barnes's medical information without the wife's consent, and she was aggressively withholding it. As the police chief had indicated, the army wasn't spending any real effort trying to compel her, primarily because *their* investigators had all the details they wanted through Barnes's role in the clinic. It was just the police and the public left out.

That put some real pressure on Katie's morning. She had an appointment to meet the wife at her home in the suburbs, about an hour from then. Reed signed off with an apology, saying he would like to accompany her for the interview, but he had to meet with the army officer coordinating the clinic's research. Katie slipped into her jeans, pulled a gray sweater over a green t-shirt, and then slipped out into the hall.

Before she pocketed her handheld, she pulled up Reed's handheld activity, just out of curiosity. He had obviously called her on his drive home last night and apparently been up doing his research for another half hour after that. He had set an alarm at 5:37 a.m. for six thirty, and he had an appointment at the military base at eight thirty. She shook her head, wondering how he would handle it.

Then his voice spoke from her right shoulder. "Whatcha reading?" She looked up with a blush just as he recognized his own details. He chuckled. "Spying on your boss?'

"Just wondering how you're going to handle a full day after the night you had."

He lifted a white hotel mug to her in answer and took a long sip before he said, "Strong coffee." He took another and then nodded to her. "Come on, they've got a decent breakfast downstairs, and you've got a few minutes before you need to head out."

She grabbed a bagel while he helped himself to the scrambled eggs, then they sat across from each other at a tiny table while he idly scrolled through a World Events news feed. She just watched him. His eyes were sharp and clear. He seemed relaxed, collected, and there was no sign of weariness, let alone the emotional wreck he'd been getting off the airplane yesterday. Eventually, she couldn't contain herself any more. "What's gotten into you?"

"Hmm?" He glanced up at her, then blanked his handheld. "What do you mean?"

"You're operating on an hour of sleep. You were a total mess yesterday afternoon, if you'll excuse my saying so. But right now, there's no sign of any of that."

He tilted his head, considering, and then shrugged. "I'm working," he said. "I guess Rick taught me that. Going without sleep barely fazes me. Having to defend my loyalty, to answer for my friendship to a man barely six weeks dead, that's...that's not easy for me. But I'm good at my job." He tapped his handheld to get the time and nodded. "I've seen the same from you."

Katie laughed. "I don't do well on an hour's sleep. I sure don't do this well!" She waved at him, his pressed suit, his perfect tie. "Anyway, I got your message, and listened through it. I think there's a pretty good chance I can get the wife to cooperate."

"Don't be too sure," Reed said. "Dora has put in some serious time working on her, and she's gotten nowhere."

Katie snorted. "Dora has a certain way about her." When Reed just looked blank, Katie sighed. "She's not good with women. I've seen it before, especially the kind of girl who gets to a position of authority like that." Reed frowned, and Katie blushed. "Fine, whatever. I'm telling you, this lady doesn't know how to talk to women. She would've put Mrs. Barnes on the defensive from the start, and that's no way to get access to private information."

Reed sat back in his chair, a thoughtful frown dragging down a corner of his mouth. After a moment, he shrugged one shoulder. "There's a little bit more there. Dora likes the wife for the crime."

"What?"

"She thinks Mrs. Barnes might have done it. There's a financial motive, and it's very specific to his situation. You saw the setup they had at the clinic? As long as he's showing real brain function, the army has committed to keeping him on staff. Full-pay, full medical expenses. If he'd been killed, she'd be looking at a moderate life insurance settlement right now, but this coma he's in...it's a full paycheck. Long-term, it'll pay out ten times what his life insurance would have."

Katie thought about it for a moment, chewing her lower lip, then shook her head. "That doesn't make sense. Without the coma, he'd be bringing in the same paycheck, right? And she'd still have her husband. Well..." She thought about his short evenings and his long days at the office. "Sort of."

Reed shrugged. "Maybe there's trouble at home. Maybe he wasn't such a safe bet, long term. Or maybe it's all nothing, but I want you to see what you can find out. Given the curious nature of his current situation, it's worth at least looking into."

"Will do," she said. She wadded up her napkin and wiped off her spot at the table, then jumped to her feet. "Okay," she said, "I'm off to see what I can see. Good luck with the men in green."

He smiled back at her. "I'll be in touch."

It was a twenty-minute drive to the Barneses' household. Katie spent it dividing her attention between the breathtaking vistas outside her window and a replay of Reed's late-night message. Knowing what she knew now about the chief's suspicions, Katie could hear the subtle hints of it in Reed's message. It was in phrases like "stubborn refusal to cooperate," and "withholding crucial evidence." Katie wasn't ready to adopt Hart's conclusions, though. The woman was protecting her husband's privacy—and he was one of the last men left in the world who really had any worth protecting. That didn't exactly sound like a crime to Katie.

She felt that all the more strongly when the car pulled to a stop halfway down a suburban street, and she climbed out into the bright morning sunlight at the end of a well-tended gravel walk. Mrs. Barnes stood waiting in the doorway, and she gave a friendly wave when Katie met her eyes. "Come on in," she called, "I've got some breakfast on the stove."

Just inside the door, Katie let out a contended sigh at the mixed aromas of cut wood and freshly baked cinnamon rolls. A fire crackled on an open hearth, welcome glow of warmth on the chilly morning. The walls were paneled in stained oak, the floors thickly carpeted with a deep blue pile. A stairway in the left-hand wall climbed to the living quarters, while the wall opposite the door was given entirely to dark-tinted picture windows that gave a shadowy panorama of the Rockies climbing into the sky.

Katie followed Theresa to the right, up a step into the open dining room, and beyond that into a sprawling kitchen. Here the walls were painted sky blue, and the tile was white ceramic. Following Mrs. Barnes into the kitchen was like stepping back out into the brilliant spring morning after the rich, dark tones of the sitting room.

Mrs. Barnes went straight to the stove, snapping the burner and the broiler off with two sharp twists of the wrist. She moved a frying pan full of scrambled eggs off the hot stovetop, then pulled a tray of cinnamon rolls out to cool. She took two china plates from the upper cabinet and turned to Katie with a smile.

"Can I tempt you?"

Katie smiled. "I really shouldn't. Besides, I ate at the hotel."

"Oh, pshaw!" She waved dismissively and started preparing both plates. "That fake stuff? No. It was probably grown in a vat. You need to have a good meal in you."

Before Katie could object further, Mrs. Barnes scooped up both plates and directed her with a nod toward a cozy breakfast nook at the far end of the kitchen, sunlight pouring in through three windows.

"So," she said, sinking into a spindle-backed chair and pushing Katie's plate across the table. She raised an eyebrow, almost demanding, and Katie finally sank down across from her.

The other woman continued in a pleasant voice. "I understand you wish to press forward with my husband's investigation." She raised her eyebrow again. "Eat! Eat!" Again Katie relented, more to her own stomach than to the woman's urging. She took a bite of the sticky bun and rolled her eyes in delight.

"Oh," she said. "So good!"

"Thank you," Mrs. Barnes said, matter-of-fact. "Try the eggs. That's cayenne and just a drizzle of maple syrup. You'll love it." She watched until Katie took a bite then nodded once, satisfied. "Good," she said. "Now, Agent Pratt, as you can see, I'm a gracious hostess. I would love for you to spend some time here this morning, learning everything you can about my amazing husband. But if you've come here to get medical access to his body..." She leaned forward, hands clasped on the table, and her eyes flashed. "Then you've wasted your time."

Katie wiped her mouth with a silk napkin and set it aside, then she met the woman's eyes. She smiled. She had a clever answer ready, but she set that aside, too. Instead, she said simply, "Why?"

"Eric is a hero," she said, the answer ready on her lips. "He's a superstar. He's famous." She stopped, considering her hands, and shrugged. "He's famous, Agent Pratt, because he changed the world. He cured *aging*, and now he's languishing in a coma, living on a machine." She sighed. "If I gave access to him, if I took him out of the clinic, that story would be all over the news. I can't bear that. I can't let his whole legacy collapse to a statement of irony."

Katie placed a comforting hand on the other woman's, sympathy in her eyes. "I understand your concern, Mrs. Barnes. It's noble of you." Theresa nodded with a sniffle, and Katie pressed on. "But there's a question of justice here. The police are confident some amount of foul play was involved in your husband's attack, and no matter how painful it would be to see him on TV—"

"No," she said, and her voice was firm.

Katie waited a moment, but Mrs. Barnes remained quiet, her eyes locked on her hands. Katie cleared her throat. "I'm not sure you've fully considered the implications of your stance."

"Oh, I have," Theresa said, her eyes flashing. "That little police chief of yours made herself perfectly clear."

"So you understand you're making yourself a suspect?"

"Yes. In my husband's *coma*. How is that even a crime?"

"The circumstances of his condition are suspicious," Katie said, knowing it wasn't an answer at all. "He had no medical history, nothing in his *extensive* lab work indicating a risk of such an attack, and for it to have disabled him so completely—"

"While still leaving me financially secure," the other woman interjected, her voice dripping with venom.

Katie paused, then leaned forward earnestly. "You can't ask the police to overlook that, Mrs. Barnes. Especially when you could clear all of this up by granting limited medical access just to us. Consider it from their point of view. The police wouldn't be doing their job—"

"Well they can do their job without my assistance," Theresa huffed. "And don't talk about 'limited medical access' to me! I've spent the last eighteen years married to a man who works behind the curtain. I know about access rights. You guys don't have the infrastructure to handle a medical data transfer, and there's no way you're a doctor—or this Agent Reed—so you're going to hand it back to your analysts in Washington via Hathor. And as soon as you do that, it's on the auction block."

"We can control that," Katie said, and Theresa answered with such a scathing look that a blush rose in Katie's cheeks. "Still...isn't it worth the risk to learn the truth?"

Theresa pulled away, crossing her arms in a loose hug, and her gaze drifted out the window to the mountains in the distance. "The truth has nothing to offer me, Agent Pratt." She met Katie's eyes, and the anger was gone. She just looked tired. "What I want is my husband back, and if I can't have that, I'll have to settle for my memories of him." She pushed back her chair and rose with an air of finality. "And I won't let those memories be shattered in twenty-four-hour news coverage. I'm sorry, but my decision hasn't changed."

6. Liaison

Katie rose as well, but before she could say goodbye, Reed spoke in her ear. "Katie, I've got news. Don't leave the Barneses' place."

Katie waited for more, but Reed was gone. She cleared her throat to cover her sudden hesitation, then she stepped forward, close to the other woman. "Umm...Mrs. Barnes, I understand your position. When I first arrived, though, you made another offer. If that still stands, I would like to take you up on it. There may be something we can do without medical access, and the more I know about your husband, the better job I can do." Theresa hesitated, and Katie shrugged. "So much of his life has been lost behind that curtain."

"It's true," Mrs. Barnes said with a sad sigh. She gave another moment's hesitation, and then a fragile smile. "Sure," she said. "You've already got my whole morning booked. I'll share my memories with you."

Katie smiled, then put on an embarrassed expression. "If I could just visit your restroom first?"

"Of course. It's just through there." She pointed the way, down a short hall that led to an old garage. "On the right."

Katie slipped in and shut the door behind her, then whispered, "Okay, Reed. Go ahead. What have you got?"

It was a moment before he answered, then he said, "Yeah, sorry, you there Katie?"

"Here, sir."

"Good. Listen, I'm still waiting to meet with the lieutenant here, but his assistant has been talking some gossip with me, and apparently Barnes was involved in a liaison with his liaison."

Katie's jaw dropped. An image of the doctor flashed in her mind, and she could certainly understand the attraction, even without his prestige. She sought in her memory for the army liaison's name. "Cohn?"

"That's her," Reed said. "It all would have happened at the clinic, so it was completely off the record, but apparently she wasn't too careful about whom she bragged to."

"That sounds like a short path to reassignment, if not an outright court martial," Katie said.

"Maybe." Reed sounded distracted. "I don't know about that, but apparently Barnes was a real handful, and this Cohn was the first liaison he was willing to work with, long before they started fooling around. So when they did, the higher-ups turned something of a blind eye."

"That's certainly an interesting tidbit."

"It's more motive, Katie. I know you don't like the wife for a suspect—"

"Well, she's really not doing anything to help me there," Katie grumbled.

"Regardless," Reed said. "If she learned about the affair, that could give a lot of credibility to Dora's theory of the crime." He paused, probably working on his handheld, and then said, "It's hard to get all the right readings without a Jurisprudence crime profile, but I've got one commercial personality report pegging your girl as the jealous type. We're pursuing this angle, Katie, so I need you to get on board. And I need you to get us medical access—"

"That's not going to happen." Katie shut him down. "She has agreed to talk with me about her husband, but the medical access is off the table."

Reed thought for a moment, then sighed. "If that's how it is, then you're going to have to get her to reveal something damning enough to take to a judge. I've already checked, and the affair alone is not enough. They want a Jurisprudence confidence, and I just can't rig that." He sighed. "I need you to break her."

Before Katie could object, he forestalled her. "I know it sucks. She's practically a widow, and you're not even convinced she did it. But it's all part of the job, Katie. Just remember that, one way or another, she brought this on herself. Confront her with Cohn, get her to talk, and even if it's something inadmissible at trial, it could be enough to convince a judge to give us access to the victim's medical records. Once we know what we're looking for...."

"It's not right, Reed." She sounded petulant, and she hated that, but he'd backed her into a corner. She could remember all too clearly the war of emotions raging in Theresa's eyes, and none of them had seemed much like jealousy. She was a woman deeply in love with her idealized image of her husband. "I've been talking to her all morning, and she's not a killer. She's grief-stricken. Her husband is gone, and you want me to attack her."

"Katie." He dropped his voice to a fierce whisper, still strong in her ear. "I've got a good feel for this guy from his assistant, and I don't think we're going to get anything out of the army. I really shouldn't even know about the liaison, but I caught a lucky break. If you can't get that woman to give us access to her husband's medical records, we have to push through her. There's no getting around these guys."

"All she has left is her memory of him," Katie answered back, in just as furious a whisper. "She clings to it. I know you like your info as motive, but what if she didn't know. What if she never found out? You want me to march in there and tell her he was—"

"I want you do to your job," Reed said. "Because if she did know, if she did find out, then that could well have driven her to something next to murder. Maybe she's not a killer; maybe that's why he's still alive, even if it takes million-dollar machines to keep him that way. But, Katie, if she did this, she has to be brought to justice for it." Katie didn't get a chance to answer that. Reed said,

"Okay, Katie, I've got to go. Lieutenant's ready for me. Good luck." Then he was gone.

Katie's heart pounded, her jaw clenched tight. She blinked in the sudden silence and then took a moment to collect herself. She checked the message center on her handheld, then put it away. Nothing new. She stepped up to the sink and washed her hands, trying to avoid eye contact with the troubled woman in the mirror. She took a deep breath and let it out in a tired sigh. Then she left the bathroom, but she found the kitchen empty.

Theresa's voice came drifting from the living room. "In here. Sorry."

Katie stepped through the doorway and found Mrs. Barnes perched on the couch. She had her feet tucked up under her, leaning to her right, and Katie couldn't help remembering the short time she'd spent in HaRRE, spying on Eric at home. The memory of him she'd seen would have been sitting right beside Theresa now, propping her up, her shoulder resting lightly on his chest, while he watched the now-dark TV. Katie could see the happy family clearly. She sighed.

Theresa seemed to pick up a hint of Katie's mood. She sighed, too, and looked around the room. "This was Eric's favorite place. As much time as he spent at the clinic, he loved it here. He loved this whole house, but this spot especially." She stared at the fire for a while, lost in her memories, then looked over her shoulder at Katie with a tight smile. "Come on," she said, and patted the cushion next to her, opposite the ghost of her husband. "Grab a seat. We'll reminisce."

Katie had to force herself to take that first step forward. Once she was moving it was a little easier, and when she came abreast of the couch she saw the photo album open on Theresa's lap. Not a digital photobook, but an old-fashioned album full of developed pictures, carefully arranged on decorative backgrounds. Katie's mom had kept books like that, years ago. With a sense of mingled fascination and dread, Katie sank down next to Mrs. Barnes. "What's this?"

"It's our wedding album," she said. There must have been forty pages, thick plastic covers bound together in a three-ring binder with a three-inch spine. She flipped all the way to the back of it. "Our first year, really. This is the last time he was really mine." Three pages from the back of the book was a two-page spread showing a younger, softer Eric receiving his doctorate at Princeton, and then sometime later shaking hands with an army officer in dress uniform. By the background, Katie was ready to guess the second picture was taken on a military base, probably the one right here in town. Below that, in the bottom right corner, was a photo of a huge empty room, cabinets lining the walls. Katie stared at it for a moment, and Theresa watched her. It was a single floor with no tables, but the size was just about right. She caught Theresa watching her eyes.

"Is that the clinic?"

Mrs. Barnes nodded. "Seventeen years ago. Before they expanded it to put in Eric's track. I used to have a photo of the grounds outside, too, and that was before the processing center went up on the northwest corner. It was a rose garden back then, that whole corner."

Her breath caught, and she shook her head.

Katie said, "How did you get those photos?"

"I took them with my phone. Do you remember—" She stopped with a tight smile, and wiped the tears from her eyes. "Sorry. That was way before Gevia. I still wasn't *supposed* to take pictures, but I was sneaky, and they weren't quite as careful back then."

Katie turned the page and found a handful of photos of young Eric at work. Most of them showed him sitting in front of a computer monitor in a tiny home office in a much smaller house, wire-rim glasses perched on the bridge of his nose. One had him in the cramped living room, walls done in garish old-lady wallpaper, but sprawled on the same couch Katie and Theresa shared now. In the photo he had open books and bound papers all around him, filling the couch from one end to the other and crowding around him on the floor, too. An old laptop computer sat open on his knees. His head lolled back, though, and his jaw hung comically open. He was sound asleep. Katie snorted in surprised laughter.

"I bet he loved that picture," she said.

"He didn't mind too much," Theresa said, the warm honey of admiration rich in her voice. "That's the night he completed the cancer vaccine. He went to work the next day and finished the formula. It hasn't changed since then."

Katie looked at the picture again, trying to grasp the man's genius. "He was amazing," she said softly.

"He was," Theresa agreed. "And he still is, Agent Pratt." Katie blushed at the rebuke in the other woman's voice. "He's not dead. He's alive, in his bed. No, he can't speak with us, he can't...can't come home. Home." She stammered, and wiped away tears again. "But he isn't dead."

Katie held up her hands to calm her. "Mrs. Barnes—"

"No," she said, leaping to her feet. She paced the carpet, right in front of the couch. "His *mind* is alive, Agent Pratt, and that's what matters. For some men that wouldn't be true, but Eric...that's all he needs. I don't care if it takes machines to eat and breathe for him. As long as his brain is working, he's every bit the man he was."

"I understand that, Theresa—"

"I don't think you do!" The other woman stopped pacing, right in front of Katie, and towered over her. "Because you're here investigating his murder. You won't say that, not out loud, but that's what you're doing, and that's what kills me. You, and that pompous police chief, and even the army doctors. You're all acting like he's dead—"

"Have you seen the army doctors' report?" Katie said, soft but firm. "It's light on the details, Mrs. Barnes, but they made it pretty clear his chances of coming out of this—"

"It doesn't matter!" Theresa shouted. She fell back down on the couch beside Katie and buried her face in her hands. "He's him!" she wailed. "I can't just forget that. Maybe he's dreaming. Maybe he's making up new stories, or maybe he's still toiling away, fixing all the strange infirmities of man. Whatever it is he's doing, he's *alive*, and I can't just forget that." She let out a tortured breath. "You can't imagine what a nightmare it is to live like that, with someone you love so close and yet completely out of reach."

A cruel silence fell, and after some time Katie broke it with a quaking voice. "Actually," she said, then stopped to take a deep breath. "I can." She waited a second for Theresa to look up, curious, and then Katie nodded to her. "My dad has been in a coma for several years now. I understand what you're going through."

"How...." She shook her head, a desperate look in her eyes. "How do you deal with it?"

"Me?" Katie barked a bitter laugh. "Not well. I spend about half my time wishing my mother would just let him go, and the other half of my time on the phone with him pretending nothing's wrong."

Theresa looked away, unable to meet Katie's eyes, and Katie knew she was thinking about the first of her reactions. It sounded cruel when she said it out loud, but keeping him alive wasn't doing anyone any good. She placed a hand on Theresa's arm. "It's not the same situation. Your husband is special—"

"No more than your father is to you, Agent Pratt. Or to your mother." She took a deep breath and let it go, then made herself meet Katie's eyes. "We have two children. A son and a daughter." Katie nodded. She'd read that in the casefile. "Jim was here for ten days. Rose was only here for two. They couldn't stand to see him like that."

"I was the same way, with my dad. I kept saying I had pressing work, but...I just couldn't handle it." She leaned closer. "It gets better, though. Give them time. They'll come back."

"I know." She gave a shuddering sigh, and then a pathetic smile. "I'm sorry, Agent Pratt. I haven't really had anyone—"

"I understand." Katie sat back, remembering Reed's stern orders, and she shook her head. "This isn't fair, Mrs. Barnes. It's not right that you and your children should have to go through this. I intend to do everything in my power to find out who is responsible."

"Eric would laugh you out of the room for saying that." She rose and went across the room to fetch some tissues from a low shelf and came back dabbing at her eyes. "Bodies are imperfect machines, Agent Pratt. Even with all the advances we've made, bodies still have flaws, and trying to place blame for mechanical failures—"

Katie shook her head. "My dad fell into a coma because of a rookie doctor's stupid mistake. He had heart problems, and they put him under for a surgical procedure—this was years ago—and then, when the surgery was over, he didn't wake up. He just never woke up." It was Katie's turn to rise now, agitated. "That was a medical error. He was already an old man, and something about the sedative damaged his brain beyond what it could recover. I can guarantee you, there's nothing like that in your husband's case. It would have made it into the army report." She gestured emphatically. "They want this done with, Mrs. Barnes, and if they could put the matter to rest, they would. The fact that they haven't.... Theresa, there has to be something more going on here."

"You know...." Theresa said, rising slowly and stepping up to Katie. "I understand you now, Agent Pratt." She was only a few years older than Katie, but she spoke like a mother comforting her child. "I understand why you're here, why you're so concerned about the case. Because you're searching for some reason behind your pain." She smiled, but her eyes were sad. "You'd be better off learning to live with the grief."

"No, Mrs. Barnes—"

Now she chided. "Child, don't drag my husband's name through the mud just because you're suffering."

Katie tilted her head, confused at the sudden hostility, and she shook her head. "No, you totally misunderstand me."

"I don't think so," Theresa said. "You're not going to find your answers here, and I've already told you I don't want answers. If I'd understood, if I'd known about your situation, I would never have met with you at all."

Katie gaped. "You really believe that's entirely up to you?"

"If you're talking about the police chief and her idle suspicions—"

"Idle? They're anything but," Katie said, bristling. "Mrs. Barnes, she is set on bringing you in, and my boss would be a half step behind her. I'm your only champion here."

"Oh, please," Theresa said, rolling her eyes. "I'll take my chances."

Her patience gone, Katie shouted, "Why?" Theresa fell back a step, eyes wide, but Katie chased after her. "Why do you insist on making yourself a suspect? Why won't you give me anything to work with?"

Theresa stopped retreating and stood her ground. "Because I have nothing to hide." She took a deep breath. "Because I won't let them bully me. Let them say what they want, let them do what they can, but I won't help them stomp on my husband's legacy. They owned him, everything but the *shred* he reserved for me. He gave himself up for them, and now they want to take what was left."

"They will," Katie said, her voice barely more than a whisper. She couldn't make herself meet the other woman's eyes. "Mrs.

Barnes, I don't believe you could have done anything to hurt him, but they won't listen to me, and you have given me nothing." She saw Theresa stiffen, stubborn, and knew she was no closer to agreeing now. Katie sighed. "They have...what they believe is evidence against you. I wanted to shield you from it—"

Theresa interrupted her. "My husband lived his life in secret, Agent Pratt, but I have not. I'm not afraid of anything they've got."

"They...." Katie's shoulders fell, her breath escaped her. Then she looked Theresa square in the eyes. "They believe Eric and Ellie Cohn were involved in an affair."

Theresa flinched as though Katie had struck her, but she gave no other response. Katie raised her hands, helpless. "They think you may have discovered it and lashed out in jealousy. They think it means motive. I'm sorry, Mrs. Barnes, I wanted to keep this—"

"Stop," she said, and there was a gentleness in her voice that surprised Katie. She raised a hand. "Just stop. I...I already know. You can stop explaining."

Katie fell quiet, unsure what to say next. Theresa broke the silence.

"I do know about it, but I've known for a long time. I...could probably find some evidence of that somewhere. If that would help. But, God help me, if this information gets out..."

"I understand, Mrs. Barnes," Katie said. She saw her opportunity there and knew what she was supposed to do. "You have worked so hard to protect your husband's reputation." She could use that. Reed would expect her to. "But if they have to bring a warrant against you, if they have to present that information as evidence to the court, it won't be a secret for long." She said it matter-of-factly, unwilling to press the threat. If Reed wanted to play dirty, he could come here and do it himself.

Theresa's mind was on something else, though. Katie looked up to see if she had considered the implications of her words, and just caught the other woman's eyes grow wide. "Ellie!" she said.

Katie frowned. "What?"

"It's...if there *is* something amiss, Agent Pratt..." She trailed off, unable to complete her sentences. She fell down on the couch, her eyes unfocused. "I still can't believe..." She faded away again, then looked up at Katie suddenly. "Agent Pratt, if someone is responsible, it could well be Ellie Cohn."

"Under the circumstances," Katie said, "we're going to need a lot more than just your suspicions. Do you have anything specific in mind?"

"He...he was with her the day before his accident." Katie's eyes grew wide, and Theresa looked away. "He has his weaknesses, Agent Pratt, and I was not willing to give him up over a little indiscretion." She sighed. "I wasn't willing to let him go away, either. So I...kept an eye on him."

"You hired a service?"

She nodded. "Snoopy. It's a local company, designed by a guy I knew in college. It's...discreet. I didn't have to listen in on...everything." She shuddered at the thought of it. "But it flagged certain conversations. It's designed to track significant changes in the relationship, and I just kept waiting for it to message me and say he was ready to run away with her."

Katie sighed. "Please tell me it didn't."

Theresa shook her head and reached up to wipe away a tear. "No." The word escaped her like a squeak. She took a breath. "No, and I couldn't even be satisfied with that, because I knew he did most of his carrying on at the clinic, out of sight of Snoopy and everyone else." She rose, and came back to stand close to Katie. "But sometimes they met in a hotel room, some dirty dive. And they were there the day before his accident. I got a message then."

She choked up, and Katie couldn't control herself. "What was it?"

"He broke it off. He told her it was over." She took a deep breath, and let it go. "I knew. I got the message almost immediately, and I'd heard the recording from his own mouth before Eric even got home that night. And when I got the call the next day, about him being hurt, I just thought how unfair it was. I never even considered—"

"She might have been angry."

Theresa nodded. "I knew. I *knew*, even then, but I couldn't put the two together." A tear escaped her eye, and then a stream. "God, how could I have been so stupid? I should have done something. I should have said something."

"There's no reason you should have suspected—"

"Pshaw!" Her voice was rough now, her grief raw. "She's a violent woman, Agent Pratt. Just look at her record. I certainly did. When...when it first happened, I was obsessed about it. When I first found out, I mean. And I dug up everything I could about her."

"When was that?"

"Three years ago." Katie gaped, and Theresa nodded through her tears. "We had a fight, and he said it was over, and we went on with our lives. Then a few months later it just sort of happened again. He still had to work with her, and neither of us was willing to risk news getting out by pressing for that to change."

"And you just learned to live with it." Katie had seen that more than once.

"How many people get married at all anymore, Agent Pratt?" Theresa cried. "I thought we could make it work. Even afterward I thought we could make it work."

"But he kept going back to it," Katie said.

"It wasn't his fault." She reached for the tissues again and blew her nose noisily, but she couldn't stop the flow of tears. "They did it to him. He was famous. He was one of the most special people in the world, and they locked him up in that place, and they just kept erasing everything he did, trying to pretend he didn't exist. He was their prisoner, and anything he could do to feel free...."

"Mrs. Barnes, you realize everything you're saying—"

"It's not fair!" Theresa wailed. "We gave up so much for them, for *her*, and then she did this? And I just kept quiet. I knew. I *knew* what she was capable of. I knew what had happened, and I didn't say a word."

Katie stared at her, fascinated, and the word escaped her, "Why?"

"Because that's what we did. Both of us. We kept their secrets for them." She wiped away her tears, sniffled once, and then fell silent, though her chest still heaved. She met Katie's eyes, and hers were blazing bloodshot. "I've done it for so long, it never occurred to me to do anything else."

"Mrs. Barnes," Katie said, her voice soft, "what are you saying?"

"I'm saying it's a sham." Theresa's breath escaped her as she said it, and then she looked around sharply as though she expected soldiers to come bursting in through the windows. She lifted her chin, though, and met Katie's eyes. "All of it. It's a lie. He gave up everything to help them maintain it, and then they let her throw his life away." She stepped away, up into the dining room where her handheld was resting on the corner of the dining table, and came back with a look of serenity on her tear-streaked face.

"I'll give you medical access. I'll give you anything you want. I'm not protecting them anymore."

7. The Secret

Katie hesitated for just a moment. Then she stepped close and pulled out her handheld. She checked on the protocol, which she already had bookmarked. "Here's what I need you to do," Katie said. "Just say, 'Hippocrates, grant the FBI full investigative access to my husband's records and condition.'" Theresa shook her head, exasperated, but she repeated the exact phrase. Katie nodded. "Good, good. Now, I also need a copy of that recording—"

Theresa placed a hand on Katie's arm, and caught her eyes. "Agent Pratt, you need to slow down and think about what you just heard." She cocked her head to the side. "In fact," she said with half a smile, "I'll give you a minute to do just that. I could use a cup of tea."

She slipped past Katie and headed to the kitchen. Katie watched her go, confused, then followed her a moment later. Clouds filled the sky outside, leaving the bright room a murky gray. Katie felt lost. "What do you mean?"

"I mean," Theresa called over her shoulder as she dug for a teapot in a bottom cabinet, "that I just let you in on one of the biggest secrets this world has ever known, and all you're interested in is your case."

Katie frowned. "You said they used him—"

"I said it's a sham." Theresa *tsk*ed. "I guess you thought I meant the working conditions. No, no. I mean all of it. *All* of it. Gevia is a lie."

Katie just stared. Eventually, she said, "Gevia?" She thought back to her trip to the doctor earlier that year. It had been a big to-do, three shots over the course of nearly two hours, and then an entire afternoon waiting around at the hospital for observation. It was supposed to be good for ten years, though. Her jaw fell open, her eyes wide. "The life extension is a lie?"

Theresa pointed a finger at her. "Not...not exactly." She nodded toward the breakfast nook again. "Why don't you have a seat, dear. I think you're going to need a little something to drink, too."

She came to the table a few minutes later with two delicate china teacups on saucers. She sank down opposite Katie, and Katie was surprised to see new tears welling in her eyes. There was no trace of them in her voice. "There's sugar in the little wooden box by your hand there, in case you need it."

"Mrs. Barnes," Katie said, "are you...are you okay?"

"I'm fine," she said with a little sniffle as raindrops began to patter against the window. Theresa put a reassuring hand on top of Katie's as she met her eyes. "Dear, I've been holding this in for years. I've never told a soul. It's terrifying, in a way, but like I said, I'm done helping them."

"But what are you telling me?"

"Gevia doesn't do anything." Katie opened her mouth to ask for more explanation, but Theresa held up a hand to stop her. "*Gevia* doesn't do it. Our other medicine does."

Katie furrowed her brow, trying to find meaning in those words, but she finally shook her head. "I don't—"

"Look, it's like this. The worst effects of aging are what? Mental deterioration, physical decline, and eventually a general susceptibility. There's...lots of things that go into making those happen, but the worst effects are pretty apparent, and they've received a *lot* of attention over the years." She sat back. "You remember Alzheimer's. You're not too young for that. Alzheimer's used to be the bogeyman waiting in the dark for old people. Total mental decay."

Theresa shook her head. "Don't get me wrong. I'm not making light of it. I lost my mother to it, and that was barely a year before they started human trials for Recollex and Zinafin. But when they got those working, they didn't just cure Alzheimer's. They improved brain function." Katie nodded. She knew where this was going.

"I get my shots," she said.

Theresa nodded. "Everybody does," she said. "And you get your strength booster. That started out as a preventive against geriatric frailty, which used to constantly cause the elderly to suffer broken bones from minor trips and falls. But everyone takes it now. It improves coordination, muscle response, and encourages bone regeneration. Makes you stronger." She laughed. "Like Popeye's spinach, my dad used to say. Eric got him into the early trials for that, and it probably saved his life. Now you and I take it to save on gym memberships. But it works. It keeps us strong."

"Yeah," Katie said. "But it's no Gevia."

Theresa's lips tightened. "That was the start of it," she said. "Then they started digging deeper. It was the third cancer vaccine that really cured aging. That was the *real* Gevia, and Eric is the one who made it happen." She smiled more earnestly this time, though the tears were back. "You saw the picture."

"I did," Katie said.

"This you may be too young for, but Eric remembered. The first cancer vaccine came out nearly thirty years ago. It was...clumsy. It helped, but we're talking statistical probabilities there, not a real cure. Not a pill that makes a person better. But before that first vaccine even entered human trials—and you can bet it did, and it made somebody a real load of money—before it even entered trials, everyone was calling it the 'first cancer vaccine.' Everyone knew there had to be something better."

Katie nodded. "I do remember this. I studied it. And the cure came out in the twenties, but it..." She trailed off, trying to remember her history, and her eyes grew wide when she did.

"It made people older," Theresa finished for her. She took a sip of her tea. "Well, it made them age too quickly." She shook a finger at Katie. "The news made it seem like some nightmare scenario, I remember, but Eric says they knew it would do that. Back when they made the first vaccine, they knew the second one would do that. It has to do with telomeres and gene shortening, and you lose a little bit of your genetic blueprint every time your cells divide. That's one of the things that makes people older."

Katie nodded. She had an uncle who had taken the time to explain it to her in detail, a very long time ago. "Something about the immune system," she said. "The system that makes people age is the same one that fights off cancer."

"Exactly," Theresa said. "And everyone who worked on the second vaccine knew that. It was all rooted in perfectly clear genetic science. It was a risk those early testers took knowingly, willingly." She smiled proudly. "But Eric thought it was a tragedy. He never lost anybody to it, thank the Lord. It was just something in his heart that told him he had to find something better. Everyone was happy with a ninety-nine point however many nines success rate, even if it meant advanced aging, but Eric said there had to be something better." Another sip, another proud smile. "He found a way to preserve total telomere strands while adapting the mutagen-targeting attributes of the second vaccine, and developed a third one that cured cancer without the side effect."

Katie nodded. "Aging."

"Not..." Theresa sighed. "I'm not a scientist, okay. I'm not. But it's not *all* aging. All metabolism introduces decay, but the big bad wolves of aging were mental and physical decay, and then the loss of genetic information that was crucial to maintaining a functioning copy of *you*. Between the mind boosters, the body boosters, and the third cancer vaccine, we had all of those conquered over a decade ago. And by all accounts that should have bought humanity enough time to figure out what they needed to cure the rest of the nasty little ailments inflicted by time."

"Then what's Gevia?"

"Gevia is the dream of a madman." Theresa said. She caught the look of incomprehension in Katie's eyes, and shrugged. "It didn't work," she said. "Eric didn't fully *realize* the implications of his cancer vaccine until later, but someone else did. Papers came out, they were discussed at length in several prestigious journals, and that's when Eric really became famous. He'd been a name on a patent application, buried beneath all his corporate, collegiate, and government sponsors, but when the debate started about his vaccine's telomerase inhibition and its likely effects on healthy adults, he joined right in and fought with the best of them." She smiled at the memory. "He was wrong, it turns out, but he was on the side of science. He always was."

Katie frowned. "I don't understand."

"There were people saying that his vaccine *should* cure aging, theoretically, but a lot of other people saying that was absurd. At the time, the vaccine was used on such a small percentage of the population and we didn't have Hippocrates yet to track things, so everything was still being done in studies. The populations were too low for any real statistically-significant analysis, but as the argument grew, people started paying closer and closer attention to the folks who *were* on the vaccine, and by all appearances they were aging normally. Gradual mental and physical decay starting at thirty and accelerating after fifty, offset predictably by their use of Zinafin or strength boosters."

Katie said, "So it didn't work?"

"It took time to find that out, obviously. But, no. It didn't work. I mean, it didn't make people act any younger, and that was exactly what Eric had anticipated in his arguments. At the time, the standard answer was that the cumulative harmful effects of metabolism are too numerous to ever fully reverse. DNA-shortening was considered just one of the myriad culprits bringing about the constant fall of man."

Katie smiled. "You talk like a poet."

"I get that from Eric," she said, then shrugged. "Well, not really. I was a Lit. major in college, but that was forever ago. I became the happy housewife, and Eric became the novelist. We never imagined that turn of events."

"I saw his books," Katie said and blushed at the look of surprise on Theresa's face. "I stumbled across them while inspecting the lab. Meg told me a little bit about them."

"Oh, Meg," Theresa said. "She's a darling." She smiled.

Katie took a sip of her tea, then shook her head. "So the cancer vaccine just did what it was supposed to?"

"No," Theresa said. A thoughtful frown creased her forehead. "I mean, yes. That's how it seemed. The debate went on and on, but as time passed and the data began pouring in, it sure seemed like all it was doing was fighting cancer. But then Eric got a call from this mystery man, a...I don't know, philosopher, really. He said he was a theorist, and *he* spoke like a poet, let me tell you. But he was a techie, too, and he told us he could resolve the telomerase question once and for all. He had his own theories, he said, but he'd keep them to himself until his little research project found an answer."

Katie leaned forward, elbows on the table. "And Eric went along with all this? Why?"

"Sheer personality," Theresa said. "The guy wasn't much of a salesman, but he was a true believer. And he was smart, too." She shook her head. "Not...nothing like Eric. Eric is a scientist, through and through. This man was different. He kept talking about prayer and the power of human expectation. He tried to give Eric lectures about the placebo effect, as though a fully-trained doctor and medical researcher wouldn't already know about it." She shook her head. "But that was his theory, and he came backed up with some impressive evidence."

"What's that?" Katie said.

"Hippocrates." Theresa nodded at the sudden comprehension on Katie's face. "It was new then, and he's the one who introduced us to it. He set up a survey in Hippocrates to track every single person who had ever taken Eric's cancer vaccine, and it told us *everything*. Every time one of them stumbled while walking, every time any of them stammered over a word they should have known. Every pulled muscle, every forgotten name at a party. It provided the hard numbers everyone was looking for, with real-time results, and it showed exactly what everyone was expecting."

She held up a hand to stop Katie interrupting, and said, "I told you, he had an experiment in mind. He brought in a huge test batch and had Eric administer the cancer vaccine to them. Most of them were told what they were getting, but a handful were told it was an anti-aging drug in the earliest experimental stages. Gevia was born in that experiment. I think Eric came up with the name, but it might have been the other one. It doesn't matter. Some of them from each group got the vaccine, and some from each group got a placebo. And you know what happened?"

"It worked?"

Theresa smiled. "That's a vague answer, but yes. To put it more specifically, the philosopher's theory was proven correct. It took three years before even Hippocrates could demonstrate it reliably enough to convince Eric, but the signs were there much sooner." She shook her head. "Those people who received the vaccine were not aging. The test proved it. At least, not seriously. But only the ones who were lied to enjoyed the benefits of it. Those who thought they'd received the regular vaccine—which they had—continued to develop symptoms of age at approximately the expected rate."

"How?" Katie asked, unable to restrain herself.

"Expectation," Theresa said. "'Psychosomatic,' was one of his favorite words. He'd say, 'The mind makes it real,' like he was quoting something." She shook her head. "No one really believed aging was curable. It was the stuff of science fiction back then. And religion, I guess. So people would take the cancer vaccine, and all those other drugs, and then there would be no need for them to go dimwitted as time went by, but they knew that was what people did. They'd watched their parents and grandparents go through it."

"So they just let themselves go," Katie said.

"Exactly." Theresa nodded. "Same thing physically. But it was not just laziness. It was real, clinical. These people's own belief in aging caused them to become frail." She sighed. "It's strange, the way our minds can work against us. We're trapped, helpless, beneath the weight of our own expectations."

"So, what?"

"So, Gevia," Theresa said. "These experiments I told you about were never published. They were run through Hippocrates with some sort of special clearance, some administrator thing, and Eric and this philosopher were the only ones who ever knew about the results." She looked down at the table. "And me," she said. "That's...honestly, that's the only reason I know any of this. Because Eric didn't believe the old man. He never thought it would turn out, so he told me everything."

"How did the army feel about it?" Katie asked, trying to guess how she might use this information. "They'd hired him to work on cancer—"

"The philosopher took care of all that," she said. "Eric thought all along he was being recruited to go work somewhere else, but when he agreed to pursue the project, this guy insisted Eric stay put. He said that the easiest way to get access to people's beliefs was to start with people who were already brainwashed to accept what they were told. And the clinic here, of course, was perfect. So he put together a grant proposal, arranged the name change and financed the construction of Eric's research lab, and then he disappeared."

"Do you...any chance you remember his name?" Katie already knew. In her gut, there wasn't any doubt. She wasn't even sure it was worth asking, but she had to.

"Martin," Theresa said. "I never even met him, and he was only in Eric's life for a few months, but I'll never forget that man. Martin Door." She seemed confused when Katie nodded. "Do you know him?"

"I know him," Katie said. "Oh, I know him."

"Well, he said *he* had expected exactly what Hippocrates showed him, and he had a plan for fixing that. He said we needed a full-scale roll out of Gevia. Everyone in the world needed to be given the placebo, the whole clinical treatment you got, as a follow-up to the cancer vaccine. Between the two—the medical cure in the vaccine and the psychological cure in the big con—we could cure aging completely."

Katie nodded. "I can see him dreaming up something like that."

"Eric couldn't even fathom it. Especially with Hathor really coming onto the scene right then. There would be no way to keep a secret on that scale, but the philosopher told him about the army's restricted access sites, and he even had something similar for himself, so that Hathor—"

"I know all about that," Katie said.

Theresa shook her head. "It was just unimaginable to us. But the philosopher said it had to be Eric. It *had* to be him because of his unique celebrity. If he would follow through with Martin's lie, he could prevent thousands of unnecessary deaths. Hundreds of thousands. The scale of it all was just huge."

"But how could they keep it hidden? I'm on Gevia, and you'd better believe I did my research before I reported to the clinic. There's not a whisper of this, and if the whole army knows—"

"Hah!" Theresa barked a laugh. "They don't. Three...four people were in on it. Eric and the philosopher, and the base commander at the time, and the president."

Katie's eyes widened. "Really?"

She nodded. "The philosopher arranged it somehow. Closed-door session, off the record, and that was a big deal at the time, because Stewart was a huge believer in Hathor monitoring."

"I recall," Katie said. "It got him elected."

"Well, he knows. He authorized the military trials and he signed the State Secrets letters that have allowed the development to continue entirely without review or oversight." She trailed off. "A few months later, that base commander died. That left three men who knew the secret and me. Well, and Ellie, probably. She worked so closely with Eric, she did the actual coverup, so she must have known."

"What about the research assistant?"

"Meg? No. Well...no, I don't think she knows. She believes in what he does completely. It's her passion, as much as he pretended it was his."

Katie looked down. "So Eric didn't really believe in it?"

"Oh, he did," Theresa said, nodding furiously. "I mean, the numbers were there. The military trials were a huge success, and at this point we've got nearly a decade of data on millions of subjects, and it's there. Gevia saves lives. Combined with the cancer vaccine, of course, but that was always the plan. There's nothing else Eric could have done, in all his life, to affect humanity on the same scale as Gevia."

Katie understood. "But it's just a con," she said. "That bothered him."

Theresa nodded. "I don't think the deception bothered him too much, but he wanted to do more. He wanted to actually do his work, release research, instead of just pretending."

"Surely he had time—"

"Oh, he did," Theresa said. "But it was all about the appearance. People were paying attention to him. Oh, when word of Gevia got out, you can bet people were paying close attention to him. Everything he did made the news, and

Hippocrates could tell us, minute by minute, how those news reports affected the success of Gevia. When he published a paper about Parkinson's detection, this story went out that the boy genius was turning his attention to other areas of study, and Hippocrates showed a one percent drop in the effectiveness of Gevia. Then Eric got involved in the debate that his new paper prompted, and I guess that confirmed people's suspicions that his focus was elsewhere, because within a week that drop went from one percent to twelve."

"That's nuts!" Katie said.

"And it was always like that. It...do you remember that guy in the Bible who had to keep his staff raised over his head in order for his side to win the war? It was like that. The reward was worth it, but the process was so silly. No...ritualistic. That's the thing. Eric was a scientist, and it bothered him that his greatest contribution to the world was going to be through this farce."

"Well, through the vaccine—"

"But that's just the thing. He arranged his own tests. He devoted some of that free time in the clinic to studying the psychology behind the placebo effect, and he spent years working on a curriculum to try to circumvent the need for Gevia. It was complicated, because the secret was so important, but at the same time it *looked* like he was working on a major improvement to the Gevia formula, so confidence soared again." She shook her head. "Nothing he tried worked, though. No amount of education or even psychotherapy could match the success of the philosopher's outrageous lie. He said maybe in a decade or two people would be so used to the idea of agelessness that it wouldn't be necessary, but we're not there yet."

"So what did he do?"

"Whatever he wanted," Theresa said. "Like I said, everyone involved in the program, in the army, thought it was real. So when he showed clinical results that proved he'd cured aging in their soldiers...oh, he became a hero. Then they started shopping the civilian deployment to pharmaceutical companies, offering exclusivity to anyone willing to honor the States Secrets letters associated with the research."

Katie whistled softly. "They thought it was real."

"Everyone thought it was real," Theresa said. "Everyone still does. They are making billions, Katie, off Eric's acting ability. And they have no idea." She waved toward the living room. "We certainly got our share of the revenue. They set Eric up really well, but it was all on his shoulders. He would watch the Gevia numbers daily, often hourly, and whenever he saw them start to slip, he had to come out with some breaking news, something to remind the world that it was working. He released a redesigned formula based on an imaginary harmful reaction to certain genetic abnormalities. He fabricated the side effect, but when he announced that the new formula for Gevia was devoid of that flaw, he saw a corresponding increase in patients' vitality."

Katie shook her head. "No wonder he started writing stories."

Theresa smiled. "That became his job, in the end. Instead of studying medicine, he was making up novel ideas that would stick in peoples' heads. That was the real cure." She sighed. "It was all this huge balancing act. He was able to chart out a direct relationship between the amount of time he spent at the office and the physical health of the national population. Can you imagine that? Can you imagine the pressure of knowing another hour spent at the office—even if you're doing nothing—would add years to the lives of ten thousand people?" She shook her head. "It was there, though. He had hard numbers to back it up. He brought in a research assistant and got a nineteen-percent boost. Just for having someone else to share his cage."

"What does Meg actually do?" Katie said. "You said she doesn't know...."

"She does exactly what she claims to do. She processes his experimental results, double-checks his numbers on the simulators, which are all designed by Eric, and show whatever results he wants them to show. And a lot of the time he *is* doing medical research still. He has made several breakthroughs in protein-coding and gene therapy work over the years. As long as it looks like something that could be related to the Gevia mechanic, he can pass it off as a product of his primary research." She shrugged. "It's limiting, and it's not worth the sheer amount of time he spends at the clinic, but it's still real science. And for all of that, Meg is there to do the grunt work and shepherd his papers through publication."

Katie sank back in her chair. "How did he manage? How could he keep that up for so long?"

"Because he had the numbers. They were his blessing and his curse, all rolled into one. The same hourly reports that condemned him to fifteen-hour days at the clinic also told him, every single day, about the number of broken bones and hemotomas he had prevented. He knew he could personally take credit for every case of dementia averted by Gevia, every life saved. Everyone who *didn't* end their days languishing in a pointless, miserable coma." She clenched her fists, and for a moment a fire burned in her eyes, but it faded. She looked up again. "He did good work, Agent Pratt. Gevia was a lie, but his efforts changed the world."

"I believe you," Katie said, and those words seemed to be enough.

Theresa relaxed, then sagged backward into her chair. She wiped her brow with a delicate hand. "So what do we do now?"

"Actually," Katie said, "I've been wondering exactly the same thing." She leaned forward, elbows on the table. "Because if all of this is true, I have no business breaking the illusion. Honestly, it would have been better for me to go ahead with the investigation not knowing."

Theresa nodded. "I know," she said. "But I had to tell someone."

"I can understand that," Katie said. "And I can understand the rest of it, too. Because you couldn't give Dora Hart access to Eric's facility when the health of so many people depends on the secrecy of his research."

"Not just that," Theresa said. "It's the image of him. Martin Door explained that on the very first day. Eric became a symbol, an actual hero, one man carrying the hopes of a nation full of desperate people. I can guarantee you a fifty-percent drop in the efficacy of Gevia by the time the world knows about this. No question. The army has been keeping a tight lid on the situation, but there has been a half-point to one-point decay every day since his attack, just because of speculation."

"I have enough," Katie said, then trailed off, thinking. She shook her head. "I'm going to have to be careful what I say, what I do. But I think I can find a way to make the army work with us. I'll need that recording." Theresa nodded. "And I'll need your cooperation. Not...you don't have to talk about this anymore. In fact, I'd advise you to keep it quiet still."

"Of course."

"And I know you are not anxious to cooperate with Dora Hart, but she's a tenacious one, and we're better off with her working for us than against us." She nodded. "Yeah." She pulled out her handheld and checked the time, then drew up Reed's schedule. "I think we can track this down, Mrs. Barnes. I'm going to go have lunch with my boss and let him know about Ellie. We'll...between the two of us, we'll figure out what to do next."

Theresa smiled across the table at Katie, and Katie put a comforting hand on top of the other woman's. "We'll find the truth in this mess, Mrs. Barnes."

Theresa didn't answer right away, and Katie remembered what she'd had to say about the truth earlier that morning. After the life she'd lived, truth didn't mean much to her. Still, she nodded toward Katie and said, "Thank you, Agent Pratt, for your concern." She sat there a moment longer, then jumped to her feet. "I'll just go grab my handheld. You should have access to the Snoopy report within a few minutes."

Katie followed her to the living room, and once she had confirmation on the access rights, she headed to the door. She stopped, just before she left. "Thank you, Mrs. Barnes, for trusting me."

"You're a good woman," Theresa said. "I can see that much. And you mean well." She sighed. "Goodbye, Agent Pratt."

"I'll be in touch."

8. Talking to Martin

Katie headed down the garden path. When she reached the curb, a car was already waiting. She climbed in and ordered the driver, "Take me to the De Grey clinic." Her next thought was to contact Reed, but she hesitated just short of making the connection. Theresa's information cleared her—Katie was sure of it—but Katie also knew she could trust a little too easily. She had good instincts, and that usually made up for her easy sympathy, but it was always better safe than sorry, especially with the chief so determined to pin this all on the wife.

So she pulled out her handheld and asked Hathor to play back the recording Theresa had given her. She expected HaRRE footage, but it was audio only. She heard the sound of a door opening, and a moment later Ellie purred happily, "You're here. I was starting to worry you wouldn't come." Eric mumbled something indistinct in response, but it did nothing to dim the woman's excitement.

"I've put myself to good use," she said, a suggestive huskiness in her voice. "While you kept me waiting. I've been busy, dreaming up grand plans."

"What sort of plans?" He sounded suspicious.

"Venezuela, Portugal," she said offhand. "We could even go to Singapore." She finally sensed his reluctance and took a reassuring tone. Katie could imagine the woman's fingertips tracing a delicate line down Eric's chest as she said, "I know people, Eric. I can keep it quiet. No one will ever know—"

"No," he said, but his voice lacked resolve.

"It's okay," Ellie said, with just a hint of a disappointed pout. "We can find somewhere a little closer to home."

"It's not that," Eric said, and his voice faltered. "It's not..." He trailed off with a sigh. Katie could only imagine what the other woman was doing to distract him. She knew Theresa had imagined it, too. How many times had she listened to this recording?

"It's not that," Eric started again, and something about his voice gave Katie an image of him pushing the woman away. "It's wrong, Ellie."

"It's not wrong," she said gently, and then more fiercely, "What we're doing isn't wrong, Eric! You know what's wrong? What's really wrong? Locking you up in a cage. Wasting all your...amazing potential...." Her voice smoldered like a hot coal on that last, and for a moment Katie believed the sentiment was genuine.

"No," he said. "No, I'm sorry, Ellie—"

"You don't just get out of it like that," she said, and all her warmth was instantly a feline rage. "*You* don't get to walk away from this."

"I am, Ellie. I am. It's over."

"It's not over!" she screamed, and that was the outburst Katie had been waiting for—violent rage, and it didn't lessen as she went on. "This is *real*, Eric. This is happening. You made a commitment—"

"I didn't," he said, trying to calm her. "I was always clear that this...it was just a fantasy, Ellie." She gasped, and he tempered his tone with kindness. "I'm sorry. I'm sorry to say it like that, but I could never really—"

Her voice fell to a heavy whisper. "Don't do this, Eric."

"I'm not...I'm not going to do anything stupid, okay? No one needs to know what we—"

"No one is *going* to know!"

"Right," he said, and he sounded nervous. "I just...I can't do it, Ellie. I can't." When she wasn't convinced he turned pleading.

"Stop and think. Really think of all the lives that would be ruined—"

"I don't care about them," Ellie said, miserable. "I care about us—you and me—and how fabulous our lives could be."

"Well, let it go," Eric said, finally with real confidence. "I'm sorry to say it, but you're going to have to let that dream go. It's over."

"But—"

"No," he said. "It's over. I'm going home." The door opened and closed, and a moment later Katie heard a grunt from Ellie and something smashed to pieces on the wall. Katie smiled at that, imagining Theresa's satisfaction to hear that bit of remorse in the final seconds of the recording, but the thought was fleeting. Hours later he would be in a coma, and all of it was for nothing.

Well, not nothing. The recording certainly addressed motive. She asked Hathor to pull it up for her in the general archive, but all she got was an error. Of course, Ellie was a database manager. It was no surprise the official record was gone. It was a lucky turn of events Snoopy saved full recordings instead of just timestamps. Katie ran the audio again, listening for the telltale sounds of manipulation, fabrication, but it sounded like a genuine recording. It was good enough for her, anyway. She sat back and said confidently, "Hathor, connect me to Reed, high priority."

The call didn't go through. Puzzled, Katie pulled up Reed's location details, but he was off the grid. She checked his history, though, and found him heading toward the clinic accompanied by Lieutenant Drake. He had only been offline for a few minutes, so Katie felt pretty confident she could catch him at the clinic.

It was still a thirty-minute drive, though. She sank back in her seat and thought over her morning with Theresa Barnes. After a few minutes she said, "Hathor, I need the audio record of my visit to the Barneses' house. Start playback at....oh, ten o'clock. Thanks."

An error tone made her frown, and she pulled out her handheld to read the message. "Audio record temporarily unavailable."

She grumbled for a moment. "*I* have audio." She checked her headset history, remembering the shut-off mechanism at the clinic, but there was no sign her headset had been disabled. "Hathor, play back personal audio record. Start at minus ninety minutes. Thanks." She got the same error again, and this time she cursed.

"What's going on?" she said. She knew the house wasn't restricted access, because she'd already peeked in on Eric there. Just to be sure, she opened HaRRE on her handheld. It showed her current location, with the camera already zoomed in on her inside the car, and when she spoke out loud to test her headset it echoed in HaRRE.

So, curious, she skimmed back to the Barneses' house, which stood in HaRRE plain as day. She retraced her steps up the gravel path and slid through the front door. Theresa was curled up on the couch, a pillow clutched against her chest, weeping in the house's emptiness. Katie quickly moved the camera to the kitchen, then skipped back in time.

Ten minutes wasn't long enough, but at fifteen an error message popped up, obscuring the empty HaRRE field. "Record temporarily unavailable."

"Dammit!" she said, and then her eyes narrowed. "Dammit, Martin are you responsible for this?" She got no answer, so she fell back against her seat with a sigh. "Hathor, connect me to—"

"Don't do that," he said, his voice a familiar baritone in her headset. "Yes. I'm responsible."

"Why?"

"Why?" His voice almost cracked. "Are you kidding me? Or weren't you paying attention?"

"It's not going to work anymore, Martin. Your little scam. He's gone, and you made him the linchpin of the whole thing. You can't fake his research with him in a coma."

"Actually..." Martin said slowly, as though Katie had given him an idea.

"No, Martin!" she said. "It's not right. Don't you see the toll this scheme is having on his wife?"

"She knew what she was getting into," Martin said.

"Listen to yourself," Katie snapped. "You sound like Velez."

"No, Katie." He took a moment, then sighed. "No, you're right, but this is different."

"How?"

"For one, I'm not killing anybody." There was some heat in his voice. "Quite the opposite, actually. Eric's wife must make some sacrifices, just like he did, but they're both doing it to save millions of lives."

"They did," Katie said. "But that's over now. He's out of the picture, and she wants no part of it."

"I heard that, Katie. It's just an emotional response, though. She didn't like you knowing about Ellie—"

"I was protecting her!"

"And you are very good at your job, but that's not my point. She'll have a good cry, she'll get over it, and then she'll realize what a colossal mistake she's made." He sounded frustratingly sure of himself. "All I'm doing is protecting her from the ramifications of that mistake."

"Oh yeah?" Katie said. "And what about me? Do you have something in mind for me?" The words were bitter in her mouth. "Some necessary sacrifice, maybe."

"What?" He sounded shocked. "No! Katie, how could you...no! Honestly, I couldn't believe my good fortune that, of all the people she could have chosen to spill her story to, she chose someone I can trust." She could hear his smile. "A friend, even. You're always a godsend, Katie."

"Oh yeah?" Katie said. She could hear the little-girl petulance creeping into her voice, but she couldn't stop it. "Are we still *friends*?"

"What?" He sounded baffled. "You can't be serious!"

"Do you have any idea what I went through? For you? And then you just walked out on me. Not a single answer, not a note, not a *word*."

"Yes!" he said, talking over her. "Heavens, yes, I know exactly what you did for me."

"Then why haven't you answered me?" She was proud the question didn't come out a wail. Her voice was level, even, but she trembled waiting for his answer.

"It was *because* of what you did for me," he said. "Katie, GAO called you on the carpet just for trying to contact me. If they'd caught even a hint that you and I were collaborating, you would have been finished. I was trying to protect you."

"Oh, gee, that's sweet of you," Katie said darkly. "You're spending an awful lot of time these days looking out for us poor defenseless womenfolk."

"Katie, that's not fair."

"You left me alone, Martin." The words dripped off her tongue like molten lead. "You just disappeared. You were the only one who could have possibly understood, and you left."

"Katie, I'm sorry—"

"I don't want to hear it," she said. "I'm in the middle of a federal investigation, and you just knowingly erased a key piece of information relevant to my case. Do you have any idea how big an offense that is?"

"I can fix that," he stammered. "I can give you access—"

"Oh, you will," Katie said coldly.

For a moment he was quiet, and she knew she had hurt his feelings. She didn't have a lot of sympathy. When he spoke, though, he sounded almost tearful.

"Katie, please, let me explain."

"Fine," she said. "Go."

"I...they're looking for me, Katie. I got a lot of new code from Velez's servers, and I'm learning...so much!"

"I'm glad for you."

"No," he said earnestly, "don't be. I have learned how to hear everything anyone says about me, and there's people saying some nasty stuff—"

"You didn't help yourself any, walking away like you did."

"It's not just your people, Katie. It's not just Accountability. It's Ghoster. He's...I don't know what I ever did to him. I don't know if I did anything at all. It seems more like he's making a power play, setting me up as some sort of villain."

"Why would he—"

"I don't know," Martin said. "I'm working on it, but he's smart. Smarter than I realized."

Katie sighed. "Why didn't you come to me? I could have...have...."

"You could have ended up in prison. You have no idea how much they want me." He sighed. "I listened to every message you sent me, Katie. I'm so...so sorry. I can only imagine what you went through—"

"Don't," she said, her voice a husky whisper.

"But I knew what it would cost you if I ever made contact."

"Then why now?" A sniffle escaped her, and she pounded a fist against her hip. "Why now?"

"Because...." For a moment he said nothing, thinking. "Because this is more important than your job, to be totally honest. Yes, that's right, more important than the woman who saved my life—who risked her own to find justice for my niece. I understand what I'm saying."

"Martin—"

"Katie, I...cherish you. I never wanted to hurt you." The emotion was gone from his voice now, replaced by the hard sound of determination. "But this trumps us both. This is the most important thing in the world. Too many lives hinge on Gevia—"

"Okay!" she said. "I get it, Martin."

"No, sadly you don't. If you really got it, you would have shut her up instead of letting her spill *everything* on the record like that. With the current interest in Eric Barnes, I was incredibly lucky to get that record cleaned before anyone else accessed it. You were reckless—"

"I could hardly censor her before I even knew what she had to say."

"Oh, you knew, Katie. You knew. From the moment you found his cabinet full of rambling fiction, you had everything you needed to figure out it was a house of cards."

"Well, I'm flattered you think I could make that leap," she said, and then she stopped. A puzzled look wrinkled her brow. "How...how did you know about that?"

"What?" She thought she heard denial in his voice.

"That incident, with Barnes's notebooks. That was at the clinic, Martin. That was off the record. How could you—" her jaw dropped and her voice rose. "Are you hiding out in the clinic?"

Martin laughed. "No." He laughed harder. "No. That would be good. But no. I listened in on your headset."

"You can't have," Katie said, shaking her head. "My headset was off. Some security procedure turned it off."

"I know." Martin sighed. "I helped design the code that did that. What I didn't know then—what I only just learned from Velez's stuff—is that a powered-down headset still records everything. It just marks the feed as private, restricting it even from the provider."

"But, wait, why would you—"

"I didn't know, when I designed it," Martin said. "No one did. No one but Velez, and Ghoster probably. In a way it's terrible, but even though the data can't be accessed directly as audio or video feed, it can still be scraped by generalized database services. Sort of like the way the unconscious mind records and stores audio stimuli to improve conscious predictions—-"

"Martin!" Katie snapped her fingers to get his attention. "Martin, this is perfect! How have you not done this already? Go back—" She pulled out her handheld and checked the date. "The eleventh. Go to Eric's attack and find out what happened. Who was there?"

"No," he said.

"Dammit, Martin, I know you're worried about the secrets here—"

"It's not that," Martin said. "There's nothing. I checked days ago. Eric never wore a headset. None of the regulars at the clinic do. There's just no point to it."

"Damn," Katie said. She bit her lower lip, thinking. "Well, that still gives us something. If something *did* happen, if someone else was involved, they knew the clinic well enough to leave their headset at home. Or they did whatever they did somewhere else, and it caught up to him later. I hate this guessing blind. I want to know what happened."

"I know you do, and I'm glad of it. But there's nothing in the record to help you."

"Nothing?"

"Not that I've found." He sighed. "But I'll keep looking."

"Thanks," she said. "Meanwhile, I've got lunch with Reed. I'll catch him up to speed—"

"What? No. No!" He spat. "You can't tell anyone."

She frowned. "This is serious."

"I know, Katie, but there's still a chance for Gevia."

"I'm sorry, Martin. I can't just sacrifice the investigation for the sake of your fraud."

"Don't," he said. "Just keep the secret. Reed can do his part without knowing about the actual physical effects of Gevia. I'm sure of it."

"And what about you?" Katie said. "What are you going to do?"

"Whatever I must," he said sadly. "I have more enemies than friends, and they all keep me busy. But I'll help however I can." He paused. "Eric was a great man, Katie. I get that. His loss cuts me deeply."

"Deep enough to make you call me, even."

"Just this once, yes." He sounded apologetic but unyielding. "I can clean the archive of this conversation, but it's no small task so that will have to do for now. Don't try to contact me again."

"Wait," Katie said quickly. "What about the Theresa Barnes tape? I still need that."

"I can get you that," he said. "Hold on. Coding. Katie is get ID Katie. Theresa is get ID Theresa Barnes. Start time is oh-nine-thirty. End time is eleven fifteen. Stream is get restricted personal audio record—wait. Break. Katie, do you need visual? I don't think I can get you full reconstruction."

"Audio is fine," Katie said. "I have a good memory."

"Good. Resume coding. Stream is get composite audio stream using get restricted personal audio record using Katie and start time and end time and get restricted personal audio record using Theresa and start time and end time." He took a deep breath and chuckled. "Okay. Album is new audio album. Artist is me. Track one is new audio track using album and artist. Do write to audio track using track one and stream."

Katie's car pulled to a stop, which drew her out of the mesmerizing flow of his gibberish. She lightened the windows and saw the clinic grounds just beyond the gate. Reed was there, standing outside the office doors and talking animatedly with the Lieutenant. "Martin," she said, "I'm here. I need to go."

"Yes, I know," he said. "Sorry. Resume coding. Track two is new audio track using album and artist. List active variables with method parameter names, details to my handheld. Thanks. Repeat command four replacing audio source IDs index one with me and start time with eleven fifteen and end time with now. Thanks. Do write to audio track using track two and stream. Thanks. Do set media access rights using album and Katie and access is true and private is true and broadcast is 'strict.'"

He spat that last out rapid fire, and it was followed immediately by a tone on Katie's headset announcing access to a new audio album.

"You shared me a record," she said, almost laughing.

"It's the easiest way," he said. "And the fastest. Look, it's dumb audio now, so you can't cross-reference any of it to Hathor—"

"But it's better than nothing," she agreed. Outside her window, Reed had spotted her car, and now he started moving toward it. "Martin, I have to go."

"I know. Good luck, Katie. I really wish you the best."

"Thank you for your help," she said.

"It's the least I could do," he said. "We both know that." He hesitated as though he wanted to say more, then closed the communication with a sad, "Goodbye."

"Bye," Katie whispered. Then she had to force a bright smile for Reed, who pulled the door open with one of his own.

"Katie!" he crowed. "I'm glad you're here. I've had a truly enlightening morning with the Lieutenant here. How about you? Learn anything new?"

She almost laughed. Almost.

9. Jurisdiction

"Come on," Reed said, holding the door for her. "I'd like to introduce you to Lieutenant Drake. He's the one running this operation."

"Pleased to meet you," Katie said as she climbed out of the car and extended a hand. The officer was a big man, six feet tall, brawny, and broad-shouldered with a thick head of gray hair. He offered her a generous smile, and she returned it. "I'm Katie Pratt."

"Nice to meet you, Agent Pratt. Your man Reed here has told me all about you."

"Has he?"

The grin widened. "Only good things. Seems like you personally kept my clinic in business." When she looked blank, he chuckled. "Saving Hathor, I mean. Not much use for a top-secret medical facility if nobody can peek in on you."

She smiled. "Fair enough, sir." She nodded toward the building. "Can we go in?"

He frowned and leaned back. "Afraid not," he said. "I was just going over that with Reed. Seems Miss Ginney is back to work already, and I couldn't crack those doors for the president himself when those simulations are running."

Katie glanced at Reed, then back to the officer. "I understand your concerns, but we need to get in there to check on Mr. Barnes's condition. We have the wife's permission."

She saw Reed's eyes widen in surprise.

Drake nodded, although he didn't look happy about it. "Do you now?" He pulled out his handheld and checked her claim. It only took a moment, and when he looked up he shrugged.

"That's...that's interesting, Agent Pratt." He nodded. "I'll have to look into that, but it changes nothing."

"With all due respect—"

He held up a hand to forestall her, and answered her with a smile. "I'm not stonewalling you here, Katie. This is all about the research. I'm sure you understand how important Gevia is, and for us to get it right, we have to follow certain protocols. That's just how it is. There's nothing I can do to get you in there right now." He clapped Reed on the shoulder. "We were about to grab some lunch. Why don't you join us, and Reed can bring you up to speed."

She grunted her acquiescence, and the Lieutenant grinned. "Great," he said with a nod toward Katie's car. "Is there room in that thing for three?"

They ended up at the same greasy spoon Katie and Reed had been walking to the night before. Ignoring the sign just inside the door, Lieutenant Drake pointed to a booth in the back corner and said, "That's my usual place. Come on." He ushered them down the row of booths, stopping for a quick word with the waitress taking orders two tables over, then slid into one of the benches and made himself comfortable, arms up on the seat back and a friendly nod toward the other side of the table, where Katie and Reed squeezed in opposite him.

A moment later a waitress came to take their orders. Katie went first, and the Lieutenant finished up, ordering a chicken fried steak with fries. Then he caught Katie's eyes as the waitress disappeared. "You've got to try one of the milkshakes after," he said. "They're awesome here."

Reed said, "Oh, yeah? Do they do malts?"

Katie had had enough talk of food in Theresa's kitchen that morning. She turned to Reed. "I've got news," she said. "Not just the medical access. I've got new information about Ellie's affair."

Reed's brows came down in warning, and Katie cut herself short just before the Lieutenant's hand came smashing down on the table.

"Damn it all," he roared, drawing looks from nearby tables. "What is it with you guys and Corporal Cohn? She's a fine soldier—"

"I'm sorry, sir," Katie said hastily, reminded unpleasantly of Rick's fiery temper. "I didn't mean anything—"

"No, no," Drake said, waving off her apology. "It's not your fault, or Reed's, either. It's Joy's, for spreading malicious rumors when she should have been busy working." He sighed. "I just hadn't realized Reed had time to pass it on before I set him straight."

Reed shrugged, but Katie spoke up. "Well, respectfully, sir, it turns out the rumor was true."

"Huh?" He frowned. "How could you possibly—"

"Theresa Barnes," Katie said. "She knew. She wasn't happy about it, but she knew about it." It was Katie's turn to hold up a hand against the officer's objection. "And there's proof," she said. "We've got Eric on the record breaking it off with Ellie, the day before he fell into the coma." She shared a significant look with Reed, who nodded his understanding.

The Lieutenant missed the exchange, lost in his own thoughts. His arms fell from their perch, and he seemed to shrink in on himself. "On the record?" he said, unbelieving. "But she was always so careful."

Katie frowned, and her voice was cold. "You knew?"

"No." The officer shook his head. "I mean, there were rumors, but Corporal Cohn was very good at her job. I've never seen better. If there's proof, though, this will end her career."

"It could end more than that," Reed said, speaking the words on Katie's mind. "Lieutenant, there's a real chance someone *put* Eric Barnes into that coma, and this new information brings a real cloud of suspicion over your soldier." Drake shook his head, but Reed leaned across the table to catch his eye.

"Do you understand me?" Reed said. "Your people classified Gevia a strategic resource. If one of your officers was involved in an action that ends up depriving us of that resource...."

Katie gasped.

Reed nodded. "That's treason, Lieutenant."

Drake nodded. "You're right," he said. He sat back and regained some of his vigor. "You're both right. I should have squashed this as soon as I got word, but the boy was doing such damn good work."

"I understand," Reed said.

"But you're right," the Lieutenant said. "This is a national matter at this point. I don't want you worrying about any jurisdictional nonsense. You can anticipate my complete cooperation."

Reed smiled. "I'm glad to hear that. Our only goal is to get this resolved quickly."

"Of course," Drake said. "And, you know, us, too." The waitress arrived with their food then, and he looked up with an expression of relief and gratitude. "Ah," he said. "Let's eat."

They finished their meal mostly in silence, and when it was done the lieutenant made a hasty excuse and departed with a vague promise to get them in to see Eric.

Katie watched him go, then turned to Reed.

"What now?"

"Well," he said, waving to the waitress, "I think we're supposed to try the shakes." He laughed at Katie's frown. "I'm kidding. We'll head to the police station. Thanks to your good work, we've just thrown the doors wide open for Dora's investigation. She'll be thrilled."

"I'm not so sure," Katie said. "This really put the nail in the coffin of her case against the wife."

Reed frowned. "I'm not arguing with you, but how do you figure? Apart from introducing another suspect—"

"It's the timing," Katie said. "Our best motive against the wife was jealousy, and we just got that this morning. But she knew about the affair for months—we have proof of that—and she had just found out it was *over*. No precipitating factor there." She frowned, thinking. "That actually takes care of the financial motive, too, because Theresa was terrified her husband would leave her for Ellie—all this time. Given Colorado's divorce laws, that was more of a real threat than anything Chief Hart could cook up. But Mrs. Barnes knew about that threat, and all she did about it was hire a private investigator. And, once again, the news that he broke off the relationship made her *more* financially secure." Katie shook her head. "No, with the timing of this, Theresa is in the clear."

"Good," Reed said, nodding. "That's good. That narrows things down for us." He cocked his head. "Why would that upset Dora?" Katie laughed, and it made Reed frown. "Katie, this isn't a vendetta for her. She's in this for the same reason we are. She's trying to find justice." He pointed a finger at her. "Don't be too quick to judge her just because she doesn't have access to the resources we have."

Katie sniffed. "I don't have much patience for any cop who's willing to settle on a single suspect with no evidence and no data from Jurisprudence. She was acting on bias, pure and simple."

"Well," Reed said calmly, "this will be her chance to redeem herself. You can measure how well she responds to new information. That's the real test anyway, isn't it?" He didn't wait for her answer. "Hathor, connect me to Dora." He waited for the connection. "Dora, we're headed your way. Katie got us access to Eric's medical records, so we can go ahead with the investigation." He paused as she said something, and Katie felt a dark sense of victory when he answered her. "No, she didn't get anything against the wife. We've got an angle on another suspect, though.

I'll tell you about it when we get there. Right. Goodbye." He met Katie's eyes with a look that told her to keep her reaction to herself. When he was confident she'd gotten the message, he jerked his head toward the door. "Come on," he said. "Let's get this thing rolling."

Katie's car dropped them at the curb outside the police station, and she looked the place over with a critical eye as they approached it. The station was a small concrete building on the north edge of town that squatted in the middle of a sprawling parking lot, surrounded by a stout black iron gate. Old-fashioned manual-drive police cars packed the lot like ornaments, shiny and impressive, but they probably hadn't seen the street in nearly a decade. The stable of new cars stood just to the right of the main building and took up considerably less space.

She stopped short halfway across the parking lot and turned to look back toward the street. "This place is set up like a fort," she said, awed.

Reed shrugged. "A lot of the old precinct stations are like that."

"Oh, I know," Katie said. "The Manhattan borough station is one of those. You could hold off an army there." She started walking again. "I'm just surprised to see it here. Boulder seems like a pretty forward-thinking place from everything I've seen."

This time Reed stopped, short of the main doors and caught Katie's arm. He dropped his voice. "There's been a Chief Hart sitting in that office since before you were born—since long before Jurisprudence came to town. And by all accounts, they've kept this city clean as long as they've been running things, so change just isn't all that attractive to them." He eyed her for a moment, then shrugged. "I guess good police work is in the blood. Your old man made a real name for himself, too, huh?"

"Jury's still out on that," Katie said, half under her breath. "Come on." She jerked her head toward the doors. "Let's find out what Ellie's up to."

The entrance to the station reminded Katie of an old elementary school. A building directory with little white plastic letters hung on the wall to the right, and a pretty young desk agent stood behind a window on her left, but Katie ignored them both as relics. The touch-screen pedestal receptionist in the center of the floor could answer Katie's needs. She and Reed stepped up to it and Reed said, "Agents Pratt and Reed to meet Dora Hart."

The receptionist screen showed a map, light blue on dark, with a dotted white line down the hall to the left and through the bullpen to Hart's office. Reed barely even look at it, heading in the right direction as soon as he heard the door's heavy magnetic locks click open. Katie followed on his heel.

The corridors were narrow, done in aged, white paint with blue, steel doors set into the walls every few feet. The doors all had security-glass windows set into them at eye level. Through the windows Katie saw a lot of empty rooms, and those that weren't empty were packed with boxes or other items relegated to long storage. A thick coat of dust covered everything in those rooms.

Katie could understand. She'd been with the Brooklyn police three months when they left their old building for a small office space in a quiet strip mall. She could imagine this office bustling, the narrow corridors crowded with all the traffic cops and beat patrolmen and grizzled detectives she remembered from her childhood. A big precinct like this might have employed dozens of people once, but now Katie would be surprised if there were more than ten on staff. Hathor prowled the beats now. Volare and TMS kept the streets safe, and Jurisprudence tracked down the bad guys. All the cops had to do was go where the computers sent them and round up the suspects. Reed's heavy footsteps echoed in the long-empty corridor. As they approached the door at the end of it, the lock snapped open with a *clok* that seemed startlingly loud.

The bullpen beyond was less stark. Half the size of the one in the Ghost Targets office, it still took up a significant chunk of the building. Katie's estimate proved a bit low, because she counted fourteen officers hard at work in the bullpen. There weren't a lot of empty desks, though, so she had a feeling this was pretty much it. A quick glance at the material open on some of those desks suggested maybe they were just trying to look busy for the Federal agents. Katie sighed, but Reed ignored it all. This wasn't his first time here. Just inside the bullpen, he turned immediately to the right and pushed open a heavy wooden door to lead Katie into Hart's office.

"Dora," he said warmly. "What do you have on Ellie Cohn?"

"Not a lot." The chief frowned, then spoke into her headset. "Carla, get me the casefiles on the Eric Barnes case. Thanks." She looked back to Reed. "Cohn is a database manager, and she's got extraordinary discretionary power here in town. Apart from some pushing and shoving when she was a rookie, she seems like a good soldier." She sat back in her chair, and for just a moment her eyes cut to Katie before she asked Reed, "Why?"

Katie answered. "She's our main suspect at this point." Hart tried to interrupt her, but Katie just raised her voice and pressed on. "I've cleared Theresa Barnes. She lacks motive."

"I don't see how you can—"

"Look," Katie said coldly. "You liked her as a suspect because she refused medical access and that was suspicious—I'll give you that. From there you made up a motive out of fantasy, and Reed dug up another, more viable one, but we've come into possession of new information that shoots both those theories to hell." Again she had to speak over the police chief's interruption. "Moreover," she said forcefully, "Mrs. Barnes has now granted us medical access and, in the process, provided ample justification for her earlier reticence."

Hart frowned. "Oh yeah?" she said. "What's that?"

"That's a private matter I'd rather not disclose," Katie said. "It's enough that I'm satisfied." Reed could have called her down for that, but he didn't. She had no doubt he would have questions for her later, but he left her authority intact for now, which left Hart nothing to do but relent.

The chief didn't see it that way, though. She looked to Reed for support, then bristled when he didn't volunteer it. "It doesn't matter," she said, scrabbling in a desk drawer to pull out a neglected handheld. "I'll just review your interview. It was around nine this morning, yeah?"

"It was," Katie said coldly. "but the record is restricted." Hart's eyes shot wide in outrage, and even Reed rounded on her in his surprise, but Katie kept her cool. "As I explained," she said, "it's a private matter."

The police chief tried to stare Katie down, but Katie was up to the challenge. She held eye contact until Hart looked away, and then she turned to Reed. "Tell her about Ellie."

Just then the door creaked open and the officer from the front desk peeked in. "Those files are ready, chief. They should be on your handheld now."

Hart didn't look up. "Thanks, Carla," she said briskly.

"Did you want to check on that before I—"

"It's fine, Carla. Thank you." Katie frowned at the chief's bitter tone. The officer took it in stride, though, and withdrew.

Reed turned back to Hart. "As Katie suggested, we have evidence Ellie Cohn was involved in an ongoing relationship with Eric Barnes. He broke it off the day before the incident."

Hart frowned, thinking, and pulled up a casefile on her handheld. A moment later she tapped some controls, and it appeared full-screen on her desktop. Katie stepped closer for a better view, but it wasn't too helpful. The police chief spoke her thoughts. "Like I said, we haven't got much. She's in the business of covering her tracks."

Reed stepped around the desk to consider the display over Hart's shoulder. He reached past her a time or two to switch to different tabs, but eventually he nodded his agreement. "That's pretty slim. Just a moment. Craig, can you get access to this desk? Awesome. Copy the Barnes casefile to it. Thanks." A moment later the desktop flashed the full FBI casefile, and Reed rapidly switched to the personal details of Ellie Cohn. Katie noticed he already had her folder tagged Suspects and wondered how much he'd already figured out. He nodded toward the desktop and said to Hart, "As you can see, we have a little bit more on her."

"Interesting," Hart said, scanning through the details—most of them apparently reconstructed by the analysts back at Ghost Targets. The police chief spoke with a faraway voice. "I wonder if she knew that."

Reed frowned. "Why?"

She pointed to the last entry in Hart's location history, and Katie immediately saw what she was getting at. Hart said it first, though. "She disappeared the same time you guys headed to town."

Ellie's official location history was certainly slim, but it showed pings just often enough to keep her identity intact, right up until Monday morning. There was nothing since then, though, for over twenty-six hours. Her last known location was at the clinic, an arrival mid-morning that had removed her from the eyes of Hathor as soon as she stepped through the gate. She'd been a ghost ever since.

Katie caught Reed's eye. "Can we find her?"

"With some effort, yes." He looked at Dora. "Can you track their cars?" Hart shook her head, and Reed nodded. "I've got some guys who can, but it's slow work."

Katie didn't know what he was talking about. It sounded familiar, but she couldn't place it, so she said, "Their cars?"

"It's a provision of restricted areas," Reed said, and Katie remembered. He continued anyway. "They have a fleet of private taxis at the clinic that don't register in the database. VIPs can use them for arrivals and departures to keep their activity hidden. Eric and Ellie both used them regularly for their commutes, and presumably Ellie took one when she left yesterday morning." He tapped that last entry in Ellie's location history. "But she clocked in when she got to the clinic. She left that record for a reason—"

"What if she didn't?" Katie said, interrupting him. She had a sudden recollection of a conversation in a private train car with Martin, and another one earlier that morning. "What if she's there?" Incomprehension showed on both of their faces, so Katie reached across the desk to pull up Ellie Cohn's map. A burning red dot glowed right on the flat gray border of the clinic, showing Ellie's arrival. Katie tapped the dot. "What if she's still there? We would never find her in Hathor."

"We will," Reed said, closing out the casefile. "Dora, bring everyone you've got. We're searching that place top to bottom."

She shook her head. "My people don't have access—"

"You do now." He nodded across the desk to Katie. "Lieutenant Drake just promised us his full cooperation. We shouldn't have any trouble at all."

Dora's eyes flew wide, but she didn't waste any time. She slipped past Reed and out into the bullpen. "All right, people, listen up. We're going to De Grey."

Katie didn't hear the rest of the call to arms, because Reed caught her elbow and steered her back toward the exit. "Hathor, Katie and I need a private car back to De Grey, now. Thanks." He tilted his head to Katie. "This should give us a few minutes alone," he said. "I need to know what you know."

It took the car five minutes to arrive, and Katie spent all of it trying to figure out how to keep Martin's secret from Reed. Dora Hart came out to the curb where they waited to talk them into riding with her, but Reed stood firm and sent the cops on ahead. After she left, he spoke into his headset. "Craig, connect me to Brian Dimms. Thanks. Brian, I need you to run a ghost vehicle analysis on the De Grey Clinic restricted area, specifically tracked departures from the clinic since ten hundred yesterday. We're looking for Ellie Cohn, who is already flagged in the casefile. Got all that? Good. Make sure I can track it on my handheld, and give it to Katie, too. No, don't put the track on the casefile. I'll attach it if anything turn up. Thanks, Brian. Goodbye."

"What was all that?" Katie asked. "You don't believe Ellie's still at the clinic?"

"A little caution never hurts," Reed said. "That process is incredibly slow, so if things don't pan out, we'll be glad I got it started sooner rather than later."

Just then the car pulled up, and as Katie moved around to the opposite door she asked him, "What is the process? How does it work?"

Reed considered her suspiciously across the roof of the car for a moment, as though he could see her attempt at a diversion, but he finally relented and ducked into the car. As she settled in beside him, he said, "I *am* supposed to be teaching you, aren't I?" He pulled out his handheld and drew up a map showing the clinic and three bright yellow dots around its perimeter, one where Ellie's location history had ended. As Katie watched, that dot stretched out into a short, stubby line creeping north along the boulevard. A moment later it collapsed back to a single point, and one of the other dots disappeared altogether.

"This is one of our analytical tools," Reed said. "We're usually using it on short-term ghosts, which leave clearer tracks in the traffic pattern than these private taxis, but the principle is the same." He gestured to the boulevard east of the clinic, the same one he and Katie had used every time they'd visited.

"Hathor has a record of all the traffic traveling along this road *except* for Ellie's car—and others like it." He pointed to the dot that was stretching north again. "We can't see Ellie's car, but we can see the car-sized gaps in the traffic history. If one of those gaps persists longer than coincidence would allow, if it continued to move with traffic in ways that a real car would move, it could easily be the ghost of Ellie's car causing the disruption. The Traffic Management System software is consistent and predictable—albeit incredibly complex—so with sufficient resources we can track the behavior of all the other vehicles on the road and find the path of the invisible ones they're all working to avoid."

The line suddenly lunged north and around the next corner to the east. While Katie watched, it crawled out to two miles, then collapsed in half, then disappeared altogether. A moment later the dot reappeared.

Reed nodded. "There are lots of false positives in a search like this. Unless Ellie did something stupid, it could take days to map any kind of path."

"Assuming she left at all," Katie said.

"Of course," Reed said. "They could all be red herrings." He tapped the screen and brought up a list of data points that meant nothing to Katie, but each one was marked with a timestamp. He pondered it for a moment, then closed out the program. "Doesn't really do any good to watch it crawl. It'll send us a report once it's finished."

"Now," he said, turning to her as he pocketed his handheld. "What's this about your interview with Theresa Barnes being restricted?" Katie shrugged, unsure how to answer. Reed said, "Was it a bluff? Because the only person with authority to clean something like that out of the database would be Ellie herself, and I don't see her helping you. So unless you've got...." His jaw dropped open, and he shook his head. "No." Katie winced, and he took it for a nod. "It's Martin."

Now she nodded once, mute, and Reed laughed out loud. "Katie Pratt, you sure know how to stir up a hornet's nest. The Steves are going to love this."

"But I didn't *mean* to," Katie said earnestly. "I had no idea, but he's involved with the clinic. He...he helped set it up. And after I spoke with Theresa he contacted me."

"You're going to tell me *that* story," Reed said, then held up a hand to stop her. "But not now. We're here." Even as he said it the car rolled to a stop. He turned to the door, ready to climb out, and froze with a sudden, miserable sigh. "And," he said quietly, "it looks like we've got trouble."

10. Truth

Lieutenant Drake stood at the gate to the clinic, staring down a throng of anxious police officers. Katie saw the clouds gather in Reed's eyes as he threw the door open. She followed him quickly.

The lieutenant wasn't happy. Red-faced, he shouted to all the police officers, but Chief Hart stood right in front of him, and she caught the bulk of his ire. "I don't know what the hell you were thinking," Drake bellowed, "but this clinic is a restricted area and so far outside your jurisdiction that you shouldn't even be *thinking* about it. When I get done with you—"

"Hey!" Reed cut him off, dashing up to the gate. He pushed ahead of Hart to confront the lieutenant directly, though he lacked two inches on the soldier's height. "What are you doing? You said we had your cooperation. Is this as much as your word is worth?"

Drake's eye narrowed to slits. "No disrespect intended, Agent Reed, but I didn't expect you to bring a stampede of dogcatchers onto my grounds. This is a highly sensitive military facility—"

"And we have reason to believe a suspect of *treason* is hiding somewhere on the grounds," Reed said. "One of your soldiers trained in escaping detection, so I thought some assistance was in order."

"Well," Drake said flatly, but without his earlier venom, "you were wrong."

"Oh, dammit, Drake!" he shouted. "This is serious—"

"Now hold it right there." The lieutenant stepped closer and lowered his voice. "Don't make this a fight between us. I *can't* let the cops through this gate, but how about you and Agent Pratt head on in to Barnes's laboratory, and we can get this sorted out."

"We can get it sorted here," Reed said, still with a full head of steam, but Katie laid a hand on his shoulder.

"Take a breath," she said softly, for him alone. "You're not going to win this one. Don't get us thrown out, too."

Reed frowned, but after a moment he relented. His shoulders fell, and he dropped his challenging gaze.

Dora bulled through him, then, and shouted, "What? That's it? You're just going to let him toss us out?"

Lieutenant Drake restrained Hart with a hand on her chest and a stern look. "That's enough," he said calmly, apparently oblivious to the angry reaction he drew from her officers. "This is over. It's a matter of military policy, not a personal decision." Hart turned to Reed, but he couldn't meet her eyes. She gave a disappointed huff and then gave the resigned order to withdraw. The lieutenant watched them disperse to their cars, which were still waiting by the curb, and then disappear up the street and around the corner. When they were out of sight, he finally relaxed a bit.

He dropped a heavy hand on Reed's shoulder. "Sorry about that," he said, "but it had to be done."

Reed only grunted in answer, but that was enough for the older man. He turned on his heel and led them through the gates and over toward Eric's lab. "You know," he said amiably, "it's still not a good time for you guys to be here, but the simulations are done and under the circumstances it seems like good PR."

"Good PR would have been to let the local police do their job," Reed seethed. "Not calling them names and leaving them on the curb like so much trash."

Drake rounded on him, stopping Reed in his tracks. "I understand you're involved in an investigation," he said. His voice was still friendly, but there was an unmistakable hard edge to it. "I understand it's the most important thing in the world to you, and I've offered my cooperation, but I'll tell you what. We do more important work at this facility every day of the week, with or without Barnes. And I'll be damned if I'll let you compromise that research to satisfy your suspicions."

Reed sneered. "What ever happened to 'Jurisdiction won't be an issue'?"

"Jurisdiction isn't my concern here," Drake said. "Saving lives is." He pointed across the lawn to the laboratory doors. "You can find your own way from here. *I* have work to do." With that he headed toward the administrative building without looking back.

Reed watched him go, then finally fell back into step toward the doors. "Anything seem odd about that to you?"

Katie had a strong suspicion the lieutenant was privy to Barnes' and Martin's secret, but she didn't voice it. Instead she said, "Maybe he didn't expect you to take him up on his offer."

"I dunno. He was pretty clear," Reed said as he pulled open the door for Katie. "That was, what, ninety minutes ago?"

"He wasn't acting unreasonable, though," Katie said. Her comment drew a withering look from Reed, and she put up her hands defensively. "I'm not saying I agree with his decision, but there was probably a real reason for it. You...I'm sorry to say it, but you didn't really give him a chance to explain."

Reed looked hurt, but he recovered quickly. "It doesn't matter," he said. "He promised us his cooperation—"

"And we're here now," Katie said. "We can do well enough without Hart's men." They were carrying on their argument in the foyer, which offered nothing in the way of hiding places. Katie scanned it quickly, then took Reed's hand and dragged him toward the lab doors. Hoping to distract him with another change of subject, she said, "How are things back home?"

"They're bad," Reed said, and he let out a sigh. "Okay, okay," he said. "You're right. I see your point. The auditors have me riled—"

"Do they?" Katie hadn't actually realized it, but it made sense.

"Yeah, and I'm letting the stress cloud my judgment." He stopped and gently pulled his hand free of Katie's. He took a deep breath and let it out slowly. "I should go talk to the lieutenant."

Katie looked him in the eye. She smiled. "Talk to me first." She reached out to push open the lab door, and waved to the big room beyond. "We can canvas the lab, and you can catch me up on things in DC. If nothing turns up here, *then* you go to Drake."

Reed smiled back at her. "That sounds like a plan." He stepped past her into the lab, and Katie followed him. He said, "Where to start?"

"Break room," Katie said, pointing across the room to a pair of doors in the opposite wall, "and the bathroom. We didn't even peek in either of them last night."

Reed chuckled and started toward the break room, ignoring the mousy lab assistant who watched them without a word from her place by one of the lab tables. Katie smiled across at her but got no response.

"Okay, DC," Reed said. "I've got Craig forwarding me copies of all the files the Steves access, and they're poking their noses everywhere."

"I can't pretend I'm surprised," Katie said. "That Fredrik seemed like a real bloodhound."

"They're not in Rick's files, though," Reed said, frowning. "They're in mine. This is *not* supposed to be a personal investigation, but the minute I left—"

"Hey," Katie said with an exaggerated shrug and some forced cheer, "maybe it's a good thing. They'll check you out real good, clear your name, and drop all this."

Reed's frown only deepened, and for a moment Katie was afraid he might admit to some misdeed. Then he shook his head. "No," he said. "I saw them dig into some of Rick's cases that were squeaky clean. I saw how they handled *your* investigation. Innocence doesn't interest them."

"Well, there's nothing you can do but wait, then." Katie smiled to take the sting out of the words, but it didn't help much.

"That's just the thing," Reed said, stopping a few steps from the closed break room door. "There's nothing I can do *here*. I should be in DC. You tried to warn me—"

"This is important," Katie said. She turned Reed to face her and caught his shoulders. "Maybe you were just running away when you left, but now that you're here you're helping me investigate government complicity in the neutralization of one of our country's brightest minds. You should be *here*. Do your job and let the rest sort itself out." A little late she added, "Sir."

He smiled at that. "You're right," he said after a moment. Then he gave a very businesslike nod. "We have important work to do."

Katie tilted her head toward the break room door, and he nodded back, then he stepped forward and threw the door open. Katie rushed through it, eyes searching. The room beyond was a cozy little lounge that reminded Katie strongly of Theresa's kitchen. Though it wasn't nearly as large, the colors and decor were the same, right down to the potted ivy growing in a basket above the sink, tendrils snaking along a decorative ledge that topped the cabinets on three walls.

An intimate little table stood in the far corner with a couple kitchen chairs tucked underneath. WorldWindows built into the walls above the table simulated a view of the grounds outside, although the panorama was considerably sunnier than reality offered. A low, well-padded cot stood by Katie's right ankle, neatly made, and a more practical restaurant-style booth stood against the wall to her left, next to the cabinet peninsula that jutted out into the middle of the floor. Reed slipped past Katie to get a good view on the other side of that, but he immediately shook his head. The little room was empty.

While Reed began a brisk search of the cabinets, Katie sighed and headed back to the main lab, looking for any sign of a stowaway. The bathroom was nearby, and as Katie turned toward it the door swung open. Katie's hand went instinctively to her gun, but a heartbeat later Meg stepped out of the bathroom. When she spotted Katie staring so intently, a blush rose in the young woman's cheeks.

"I'm sorry," she said quietly. "Was I not supposed to?"

Katie ignored the question and stepped quickly around the door and into the bathroom. It lacked the opulence of the rest of the lab, just a tiled white cube with a toilet, sink, and a clear glass shower in its corners. A wicker basket held towels, and there were no cabinets. No hidey holes. No Ellie Cohn.

Katie left the bathroom to find Reed waiting just outside. He asked with his eyes, and she shook her head. He sighed.

Meg wrung her hands, anxiety making her gaze dart back and forth between the agents. "What's going on?" Her voice came out almost a wail.

Without really looking at Meg, Reed said, "We suspect Ellie might be hiding somewhere on the base." He stepped past the bathroom door and opened one of the many huge storage cabinets that lined the walls. "These might be big enough to hide in...."

"Hide?" Meg said, her voice climbing to a squeak. "You guys are after Ellie?"

"Yeah," Katie said with a concerned frown. "The lieutenant didn't tell you?"

"Nobody tells me anything," Meg said. "Oh, god, you think...Agent Pratt, I saw Ellie. I saw her yesterday. I didn't think anything about it."

"It's okay," Katie said. "You couldn't have known."

Reed undermined her efforts with a sudden intensity. He left the cabinet open and crossed to Meg in two long steps. "Where is she," he asked, looming over her. "What did she want? Did she say anything to you?"

"N—no. Not really." Meg's eyes were darting again, to Reed in fear, to Katie in a plea for help. "She was just checking in. I'm sorry. I—I don't remember anything."

Katie stepped up behind Reed and pulled him back with a light touch inside the bend of his elbow. "It's okay," she said again, with a tone meant to calm Reed down as much as to reassure the startled girl. She tilted her head toward Meg. "Do you know what time she was here?"

Meg looked up at the ceiling, thinking. "Umm..." she said. "Ten-ish. Eleven. She wasn't here long."

Reed spoke in a gentler voice, following Katie's lead. "Did you see where she went?"

Meg looked uncomfortable in spite of his measured tones. "I don't know. I didn't think to watch her."

"But did she go somewhere else on the grounds?" Katie asked. "Did she leave the clinic, or did she go to one of the other buildings? Maybe the administrative building?"

"Yeah!" Meg nodded eagerly. "I mean, she might have gone there, yeah." She glanced at Reed and at the cabinet he'd ripped open. "She's not *here*, though. I would know if she'd stayed at the lab."

"That's not super helpful," Reed grumbled, half under his breath.

"It is," Katie said. "There are three other buidings in the clinic, but none of them are as private as this one. If Ellie's hiding in one of those, Drake should be able to track her down pretty quickly."

"Unless he's helping her," Meg said. She shrank away when Reed and Katie both turned on her, then shrugged. "I mean, those guys stick pretty close together."

"Which is why we need Hart's people here helping out," Reed growled. After a moment he nodded. "That might work, actually. We might be able to put a little more pressure on him to get into the other buildings. If we assure him we don't need to search the lab, maybe he'll let them in."

Katie chewed her lip. "I don't know," she said. "He seemed pretty determined to keep it to just us."

Reed waved away her objection. "We can do this." He pulled out his handheld and then cursed at the blank screen and dropped it back in his pocket. "I can do this," he said. "I can be persuasive. Of course, it would be easier if..."

Katie caught his eye. "Maybe...Reed, do you remember what we were talking about in the car? Do you remember that other conversation I had?" It took him a moment to nod, and in that time Katie saw Meg's eyes narrow, trying to follow. Katie hurried on. "Maybe you should just let this go, Reed."

"What do you mean?"

"I...." Katie clenched her fists in sudden frustration. "I can't explain, Reed, but I strongly suspect the lieutenant has his own reasons for trying to protect the clinic's privacy. Maybe instead of trying to get around him, you should try to work with him."

Reed frowned. "You're talking about...*him*. Oh." Martin Door. He nodded, finally getting it, then he frowed. "Katie, what are you talking about? If you know something—"

"Trust me, sir, I'd like to bring you in on this, but...I can't."

Meg gave a tiny little gasp, but Katie caught it and looked up in time to see the girl's eyes were wide. Meg tried to cover it by blinking, but Katie knew what she'd seen. The girl knew the secret. And now she knew that Katie knew it, too.

Reed saw the looks passed between the women, but he was at a loss to comprehend them. He titled his head and considered Katie. "You know I can't leave it at that," he said. "Especially given the nature of your informant and the investigation going on back in DC right now. Spill it."

Meg spoke up before Katie could answer. "You know what!" she shouted, "I do remember something. About...about yesterday. About Ellie. She was here...she was looking for something. For a file, on one of the computers. I can show that to you."

Reed started to say, "Not now"—Katie could see the dismissal in his eyes—but he stopped, then said, "Bring it up. Agent Pratt and I are going to have a conversation in the lobby."

Katie saw panic in Meg's eyes, but the girl was clearly scared of Reed. She bobbed a quick nod, almost a curtsy, and then scurried away to one of the lab tables. Reed gathered Katie up with his eyes and ushered her toward the doors.

"You're a good agent," Reed said under his breath, not slowing down, "and I'd like to think we're friends, Katie. Really. But you can't keep secrets from me."

"It's not like that," Katie said earnestly. "I made a promise."

Reed stopped so he could look her in the eyes. "To Martin, right? Dammit, Katie, that man is going to take us both down if you're not careful. You made a promise to *me*. And to Eric Barnes, and to his wife and to that frightened little girl back there, as soon as you took this case. And now you're putting Martin's priorities above that?"

"No," Katie shook her head. "I understand...look, this case is important to me. There's no way I'm letting those people down. But I'm telling you, this secret has no bearing on the case."

Reed frowned. "I find that hard to believe."

"Trust me," Katie said. "You can trust me. I know what I'm talking about."

He showed no sign of relenting, but before he could press her any further, a voice called from an intercom mounted on the wall. "Agent Reed, please contact Lieutenant Drake at the administrative building. Agent Reed, contact Lieutenant Drake at the administrative building. Thank you."

He frowned. Then he took a step away, but he didn't break eye contact. "I trust you, Katie." He hesitated and deflated a little. When he went on, his voice was weaker. "I trust you, Katie, but I'm in with the wolves now. It's not easy."

"It's okay," Katie said. She glanced over her shoulder toward Meg, halfway across the sprawling lab, and then back to her boss. "It'll be okay, sir. You can trust me."

His lips tightened in a smile, then he slipped through the door and disappeared. Katie stared at the closed door for a moment, then shook her head and turned back to Meg. "Have you got it?" Meg nodded, and Katie jogged across the room toward her, but when she got there the desktop was blank. Katie fought a smile. "There's no file," she said.

Meg shook her head, tears springing to her eyes. "I'm sorry," she said. "I shouldn't have lied, but I thought you were going to tell him...."

"I understand," Katie said. She put her hands on her hips and considered the other woman for a moment, measuring. "How much do you know?"

"More than I should," Meg said. "Same as you." There was a hint of ferociousness in her voice at that last, and Katie unconsciously fell back a step. Meg said, "I don't know how you—oh. Theresa told you." Katie nodded, and Meg shook her head. "That woman doesn't get it."

"She does," Katie said, then reached out and pushed Meg's chin up so they could meet eyes. "And I do, too. I wasn't going to tell Agent Reed. I didn't. Your secret is safe."

Meg spat the word out. "Safe." She shook her head. "Too many people know, Katie. Too many. The lieutenant knows. I think you guessed that. Ellie never should have known, but he told her. Theresa...."

"Ellie and Barnes were having an affair," Katie said, and Meg only nodded absently. "We think that might have driven her to attack him. He tried to end their relationship, and if Ellie was in love—"

Meg cut her off with a snort. "She didn't love him," she said. "No more than he loved her. It was just sex." The girl said "sex" like it was a dirty word, but there was something wistful in her eyes. She clutched her hands to her heart. "Eric tried to end it? I didn't know."

"That was the day before..." Katie trailed off, considering Meg out of the corner of her eye, but the girl wasn't listening. Her eyes were on something far away. Katie caught her attention with a hand on her shoulder, and said with a gentle voice, "You had a relationship with him too?"

Meg looked up at her with wide eyes, and after a moment nodded mutely. Katie sighed. "What is it about that man?"

Meg's jaw dropped. "Are you...are you serious? He's *Eric Barnes*. I've had a crush on him since high school." She shook her head. "But it's not even that. It's this place." She looked around, at the blank walls and the picturesque, artificial windows overhead. "It's unreal. After a while, all the privacy, all the secrecy, it gets into your head." Her eyes drifted down to her feet, but she coughed out a laugh. "It's the weirdest feeling. It's like being drunk. But...just, knowing that no one can see you, no one can hear you. Knowing that it's really, truly secret. You can't imagine the feeling."

Katie bit her tongue against the answer that sprang to mind. She said, "So you...you slept with him?"

Meg looked up sharply and then away as the blush rose again. "Umm. No." She probably didn't realize how much regret Katie could hear in her voice. "We almost did," she said. "A long time ago. It was this place. But...we couldn't. We both knew we couldn't. It would have interfered with our work, you know, and Eric's only real love was his work."

"But his work is—"

"It's not a lie, Miss Pratt. If you think it is, then you don't understand. Eric didn't just hide out in here and...and...read and play games. He was working. Always working. That mind..." Her eyes drifted away from Katie's toward the bed in the back corner. She sighed. "He's a genius."

"And he didn't choose you." Katie put just enough sting in her voice to get the point across, and Meg turned back to her with narrowed eyes.

"It's nothing like that," she said. "He loved me, and I loved him. We were friends. That...the other thing, that was a long time ago, like I told you." Her breath caught, and she forced out a long breath. "Ellie was just a distraction. An escape. There was never anything real there."

Katie frowned. "Then you don't believe she attacked him?"

Meg's eyes got wide. "Who said anything about an attack?"

"That's why we're here," Katie said. "We suspect someone *caused* Eric's current condition—"

"You do? But how?"

"With a chemical synthesized at one of these workstations. We haven't had a chance to inspect the body yet, but when we do we expect to find—"

Meg shook her head, horror in her eyes. "You...no. It doesn't work like that. You can't just make up a magical coma drug."

"But surely with all the data available on Eric Barnes, and the kind of processing power you have here—"

Meg shook her head, definite. "Nope. That's not how these machines work. It's all driven by Hippocrates. It exists to find *general* solutions, not to make designer drugs. That's an entirely different class of equipment."

Katie tucked her hair behind her ear, eyes fixed on one of the benches. "Then how did she...." Her eyes narrowed, and then she hit Meg with a penetrating gaze. "So if you didn't know we suspected an attack, what *did* you think we were talking about?"

"I...well, Ellie," Meg said. "Right?" Katie looked blank and Meg gasped at her. "You mean...you know about the attack, but you don't know what Ellie was up to?"

Katie took a step back. "I told you, we know all about the affair."

Meg shook her head. "No. No. They weren't just lovers, Katie. But you're right. If you think he was attacked, it must have been Ellie who did it. Eric and Ellie were...conspirators. Right? They had a plan." Her voice fell to a whisper on that last word and she looked around anxiously, but the two women were alone in the lab.

Katie shrugged helplessly. "I'm sorry, Meg, you're going to have to make it plainer than that. I don't understand what you're getting at."

"She was a very compelling woman," Meg said, almost offhand. "Whatever Ellie wanted, Ellie got. She had a power over people." She sighed. "Even Eric. And what Ellie wanted most was a lot of money." She met Katie's eyes at last. "They were going to do it together. He never would have done it, but that woman...."

"But what was she going to do?" Katie asked.

"She was going to sell Gevia," Meg said. "State secrets. It's treason, Katie, but that didn't stop her. If she lets it get out, no one else can make it work like we do. Do you understand? She'll get rich, and she'll disappear completely, and then the Gevia project will *end*."

It was worse than the girl knew. Ellie had *already* disappeared completely, and she had a full day's lead on them. Given this new information, the hunt for Ellie Cohn had just grown a lot more important. Without a hint of patience in her voice, Katie growled into her headset, "Martin, connect me to Reed, now."

11. The Real Crime

Katie got no answer, and after a moment she pounded her fist on the nearby lab table. "Dammit, Martin, answer me!"

Meg had ignored the first comment, but at the second her eyes went wide and she said, "Martin? Martin Door? He's not here either, Agent Pratt!" Her eyes went to the disabled headset still on Katie's ear, and she chuckled. "Oh. You're talking to your assistant. You know those don't work in here, right? It's easy to forget. My first few weeks—"

Katie ignored her. She said more sharply, "Martin, I'm not playing here. Connect me to Reed."

Meg tilted her head, curious at Katie's antics, but Katie's attention was all on her headset and the exasperated sigh that suddenly played in her ear. Martin grumbled, "I'm not a secretary, Katie, and believe it or not, you are not the single most important thing going on in my life. You can't just assume I'm listening in on you wherever you are, whatever you're doing—"

"Shut up," Katie said, and Meg blinked in surprise. Katie said, "We've got trouble with Ellie Cohn."

"I know," Martin said, a bit sheepish. "I...I was listening."

Katie allowed herself a smile, but it evaporated quickly. She said seriously, "Ellie's on the lam, and she's dangerous. Put me through to Reed. He's in the administrative building."

"I can't do that," Martin said. "And I wouldn't if I could, because I suspect you just want to fill him in. This is highly sensitive information, Katie."

At the same time, Meg spoke up. "I don't know if you're messing with me, or if you're just crazy, but it's not funny." Katie tried to wave her quiet, but the girl's voice grew frantic. "It's not funny, Katie! Everything keeps getting worse! And I thought maybe you could understand, but no! I can't take it."

"Wow," Martin said flatly. "How do you put up with that?"

"She's been through a lot," Katie said, quietly chastising, but Meg heard her and broke into a wail. Martin grunted.

A moment later a voice spoke from the loudspeaker on the wall. "Meg Ginney, you have an urgent message waiting at the administrative building. Please report to the administrative building immediately." Meg's eyes shot to the speaker, and then she drew a ragged breath, visibly taking control of herself. When she was done she rounded on Katie, who was waiting patiently.

"Well?" Meg said, demanding. "Come on. This is a restricted area. I can't just leave you here alone."

Martin said immediately, "Offer to wait in the lobby. She can lock you out of the lab that way."

Katie followed his suggestion, and Meg met it with a frown, but at the same time the message repeated over the speaker, and she threw her hands up in agitation. "Fine. Whatever."

As soon as they stepped into the lobby, the lab door fell closed with the loud snap of locks engaging. Meg used the keys on her chain to throw the three deadbolts, though, before she was satisfied. She pointed to the low couch against the wall. "That's more comfortable than it looks. I'll be back in a sec."

She didn't tarry beyond that. When she was out the door, Martin said with clear satisfaction, "Good. Glad that's sorted."

"You're playing games, Martin," Katie said, irritated. "I'm surprised you're not more concerned about this."

"Oh, I couldn't be more concerned," he said seriously. "I've had six different diagnostics running since the moment she mentioned what Miss Cohn was up to. But this is a matter *we* need to handle. We can't turn it over to the army or even Ghost Targets."

"That's not how it works," Katie said. "I *am* Ghost Targets. You and I are not a team, Martin."

"And yet you called my name." He said the words offhand, but they stopped Katie short. She stood with her jaw open, unable to respond, and after a moment Martin said, "Ah, good. I've got something. That woman is good—really good—but I found something that should make Reed's TMS analysis a little faster."

"You know about that?" Katie said. "Have you been listening in on us all day?"

"Heh, no. No. The FBI analysts tend to make big ripples when they start poking around in the database. It's hard to miss."

"You're really not sounding like one of the good guys, Martin. I know you've been burned in the past—I was there—but you have to learn to trust Reed because I can't do this stuff by myself. If you keep locking him out—"

"Not at all," Martin said. "I get it. I shared that partial voiceprint of Ellie with Reed and Dimms both the moment I got it. I'll do the same with anything else my searches turn up. As a matter of fact, Reed is charging back to the lab to tell you all about that one right now. I'd say he feels in full control."

He took a deep breath and released it as a sigh. "I just need you to keep your promise. I'll do everything I can to support your manhunt, and that should be enough to keep things moving. Don't tell Reed about your new motive, though. Hell, just let him believe she's selling the chemical formulas. Even without the secret, that will still get plenty of priority."

"We have to find her, Martin—"

"You're right about that," he snapped. "You need to find her, or all of our precautions are a waste of time. Figure out where she is, and do it quick."

Katie frowned. "Why the sudden urgency?"

"Because she's in the database," he said. "She's like a mini-Ghoster. She may not have all the same access rights, but that woman knows how to work the system, and she's going to find out you're after her. There's no way to keep something like that secret. She's *already* so well hidden that I can't find her. Once she finds out she's an active suspect...."

"I get it," Katie said. She caught a glimpse of Reed through the glass doors, rushing toward the lab, and knew her time was short. "Here's what I need you to do—"

Martin chuckled. "I'm not a database service, Katie. You can't just ask me to help—"

"This is your secret," Katie said, "and you're imposing restrictions that limit my team's usefulness, so I need you to offset that. You're going to find out what Ellie is really up to. See who she's been in contact with, off the record. Check international calls, or find out if there's other ghosts who've been in touch with her. That would be a big red flag. But right now we're acting entirely on Meg's word, and that's just not enough. Get Hathor to talk."

"I don't know," Martin said. "It won't be easy."

"I know. I know. That's why I need you to do it. Reed and I can handle the manhunt, but you're uniquely qualified to figure out what Ellie's got in the works. Once we know that, we can slam this thing shut."

"I'll do what I can."

"You can do it, Martin. I know you can." Reed was at the outer door. She sighed. "Reed's here. I suppose that's it, huh?" The silence she got was answer enough.

When Reed burst in, he found her still standing just inside the lobby, her back to the lab door. He stopped short, considering her, and said, "What's going on?"

"Nothing," she said. "Meg got called away. What was your urgent message?"

"Call from Washington," he said, and immediately waved it away. "Didn't get there in time, obviously. But I caught Lieutenant Drake and dragged some more out of him, and then while I was in the communications room I got an update from Dimms. We have a lead on Ellie's position."

"Oh yeah?" Katie said, trying to sound surprised. "She's not at the clinic?"

"Not unless she came back sometime this morning. And thank heaven for that. Let's get out of this godforsaken black hole." He didn't even wait for an answer but turned on his heel and pushed back out into the chill afternoon. Katie hurried after him and caught up halfway down the path to the east gate.

He was just hooking his headset back on his ear, and as Katie approached he grumbled, "It'll be nice to be online again. The damn silence makes my skin crawl."

Katie felt a pang of guilt at keeping him in the dark, but she fought it down. "What was it you found?" she asked, realizing Martin had never said.

"We've got her voice—or one like it—on a private headset yesterday afternoon at two twenty-two, westbound on Iris Avenue."

"Westbound?" Katie said. "She was moving? So someone was with her?"

"Nope. From the sound of it, she had the window down, screaming at the other traffic. Our hit came off a snippet recorded through a passing motorist's closed window."

"Wow," Katie said. "What was she yelling about?"

Reed shrugged. "Impossible to tell, but she was *not* a woman in control of herself, that much is clear. Seems unlikely that would be a delayed emotional outburst, after all this time, but it could have something to do with us."

Or with her attempts to sell the clinic's secrets, Katie thought. She only nodded. Reed wasn't watching her, though. His attention was all on his handheld as they left the clinic's heavy gates, and he breathed a theatric sigh of relief when the screen flashed to life. He looked up for just a moment to point Katie to a car waiting at the curb. "That's us," he said.

She got in opposite him and watched him while the car pulled out into traffic. His eyes burned with a new intensity, strong jaw clenched as he looked for the answers he needed. Occasionally he opened his mouth to mumble a question to himself, but his focus was locked on the screen. After a while of watching that, Katie looked over to the driver's monitor and saw that they were headed to the police station. When she looked back, Reed was watching her.

"Don't worry," he said mildly. "Dora won't be there." He smiled when she tried to object, then tossed her his handheld. "Hathor, connect me to Dora. Thanks."

Katie watched him, curious what he was up to. He looked serious, sure, capable. For the first time in two days, she realized, he was really in control of his own investigation. There was something more, though, and Katie suspected it had to do with the message from DC. He was wearing his authority like a tailored suit.

When Hart answered his call, he skipped the formalities. "Dora, we've got Ellie Cohn somewhere in West Boulder, possibly Crisman or Salina. I want you to get boots on the ground, okay? I'm bringing in Federal agents to help, but we're going to need everything we can get."

He paused while she responded, then shook his head. "No, I've got a rough TMS analysis painting a heatmap for us. Should be a search perimeter in your message center." He waited again, then put on a smile. "Thanks, Dora. Let me know. Yeah. Goodbye."

He looked over to Katie, then nodded to the handheld she had clutched in her lap. "Any questions?"

"Huh?" She almost blushed and looked down at it for the first time. It was the TMS analysis he'd shown her earlier, but, instead of three discrete dots on a close-up of the clinic, the map now showed all of northwest Boulder, the clinic tucked neatly against the southeast corner of the screen. A bright yellow thread tracked north and then west from the clinic for several miles. It split into three threads at one point, then those converged again a few miles later on Iris Avenue, which was the spot of the voiceprint Martin had given them.

The solid thread ended less than a mile west of that point, but the map all around it glowed with a fluid overlay of varying shades of yellow. She knew how to read the heatmap with the dark orange, mostly transparent background representing low probabilities and a handful of brighter yellow corridors snaking through it that represented the most likely routes Ellie had taken. The edge of the yellow overlay cut off sharply at a range of about fifty miles, though—a rough circle centered on Martin's voiceprint. Katie frowned.

"What's this?" she said, tracing the circle with her finger. "She's had plenty of time to get outside this radius...."

"Time, yes," Reed said. "But no power." Katie tilted her head and he explained. "For financial reasons, the private taxis don't passively recharge on the grid. They can be recharged at the clinic, the base, or at a commercial station, but all of that is monitored and recorded. That's one of the few ways the army has of auditing the use of the cars. When Ellie called for a getaway car, the system sent her a local two-seater with a hundred-mile powerplant that was already under half capacity. We can calculate exactly how much power she had left by the time she recorded that emotional outburst, so we know for a fact she's somewhere within this area."

"Her car is, anyway," Katie said.

Reed glanced up and nodded. "True, but she couldn't have gotten far on foot in the last twenty hours, and I expanded our search to account for that."

"What about public transport?"

"No good," He said. "There's no way to take the trains without exposing your identity. Same for the airports." Katie said nothing, just arched an eyebrow, but it was enough to draw a chuckle from Reed. "Well, okay, you did. That was special, though."

Katie pointed at the screen. "*She's* special."

"She's no Martin Door," Reed said. "I got the lieutenant to show me her access rights, and he provided a list of the software she uses. Between the two, that gives us a pretty good idea what she can do." He held out a hand, and Katie returned his handheld. "All told, we've got a reasonably high confidence she's somewhere on this map."

"Good," Katie said. "Then we start knocking on doors."

"Nope." Reed shook his head. "That's what the cops are for. You and me, we're going back to the station to try to figure out just what the hell is going on."

Katie narrowed her eyes. "What do you mean?"

"I mean, we've finally got the keys we need to unlock this thing, and I intend to use them." He stopped, considering, and then looked over at Katie from the corner of his eye. "You think Martin would help us out on this?"

She bit her lip. After a moment, she said, "I think he's already doing everything he can for us."

Reed nodded. "I'm putting a lot of trust in you."

"I know, sir." She hesitated, then said, "I won't let you down."

He smiled. Then he nodded to the driver's monitor. "We've got five minutes. Why don't you check out the voiceprint?" She shrugged her agreement, and Reed said, "Craig, play sample seven from the voiceprint composite of Ellie Cohn for Katie. Thanks."

A voice started talking in her ear, a happy housewife by the sound of it, chatting idly with a passenger in her car about the kids' soccer game. Katie tuned out the chatter, listening for the relevant audio in the background while she pulled out her handheld to check out the details of the file. It was attached to the Eric Barnes casefile with a red marker at the six second mark, so she was ready when the playback hit it and heard the indistinct voice shouting through the window. It was pretty clearly a woman's voice, but Katie couldn't make out any words.

The voice grew rapidly louder and then dwindled again within seconds. Another red marker flagged eleven seconds as the end of the relevant clip, but Katie left the audio playing. The housewife commented on the disturbance, "Well...that was weird," and for a moment Katie had hopes of a physical description, an interpretation, something, but the woman fell right back into her play-by-play. Katie sighed and shut it off.

"That's it?" she said. "That's all we got? How on earth could you identify that as Ellie?"

"We couldn't. Not positively. That's why it didn't show up in her location history. But Hathor gave it a significant confidence of being her—something between twenty and thirty—and from there it ran a comparison to all the other recorders in the vicinity and generated a composite recreation of the voice patterns."

"Oh!" Katie said. "Let's hear that!"

"It's garbage," Reed said. "There's no way to map it to anything useful to a human ear. There's twenty-seven different recorders in play over the space of a ten-second window, each contributing meaningfully to only a second or two, sometimes less. They all have different quality, different proximity, different volume. The voiceprint software is designed to accommodate those differences, but you and I aren't. Trust me, I've listened to it."

"Okay," Katie said. "But where are all the other recordings?"

"You can access them by opening up the composite, but I wouldn't bother. The one you just heard is easily the clearest."

"Wow," Katie said. "Well, what does the voiceprint software show? What's she saying?"

"It's unintelligible," he said. "From some of the low-confidence guesses it spit out—you can see a list of them on that tab there, yeah—I'd say she was probably trying to talk to Hathor, but nothing registered."

"Those..." Katie scanned through the list, but the longest of the reconstructed phrases was two words, "Text me," which she supposed Reed was taking for "Connect me." The rest were just phonemes, sometimes two syllables strung together, but nothing meaningful. Katie shook her head. "Why would she be shouting Hathor commands out the window of a moving car?"

"A *fast*-moving car," Reed corrected her, and reached over to change to another page on her casefile. "The woman in sample seven was doing forty-five miles per hour, and you heard how Ellie blew by her. The TMS analysis suggests she was traveling somewhere between sixty and ninety miles per hour." Katie whistled, and Reed nodded. "And there's more. It was barely thirty degrees at the time, and she had the window down at sixty-plus miles per hour so she could shout out of it. That's all very weird."

"And," Katie said sadly, "we can't even be sure it's her. What's the confidence on this?"

"That's a good question," he said. "The composite voiceprint is around twenty-eight, base, but a standard location cull of similar voiceprints bumps it up over forty. We factor in the TMS analysis already giving us a real possibility that she was there, and that gets us up around sixty."

"That's not good enough," Katie said, concerned, and Reed shrugged.

"You're right," he said. "And that's what you and I are going to be working on." He turned his handheld toward her again, showing her the TMS analysis. "If we can find her anywhere on this map, before or after that voiceprint, it could move our confidence much higher. And, for that matter, if we find her anywhere else...well, that would invalidate our partial print, but it would get us moving in the right direction."

He held up a finger as a message came in over his headset, and he said, "Yeah, connect me. Paul! Right. Tell me what's happening." He nodded, listening, and then said, "Okay. Okay, great. That's great. But I need more men on this. No." He glanced over at Katie, and said, "It's a treason case, Paul. You can do this

for me. I don't care if you have to fly them up from Texas. Right."
He nodded, and then again. "Right, perfect. Thanks. Goodbye."

He shook his head, and Katie spoke up. "What was that?"

"Hmm?" He looked over. "Marshals," he said. "I'm bringing in
marshals for support. If she *has* gone to ground—if she's
anywhere outside this circle, really—then they're the ones who
are going to find her."

They arrived at the police station then, just as several police
cars sped out of the lot. Katie caught a glimpse of Chief Hart in
one of them and felt a touch of gratitude to Reed. The two of
them went straight to Hart's office, and Reed closed the door
behind them.

"Craig, Katie and I are using Dora's desk. Copy the Barnes
casefile to it. Thanks." The desktop flashed to life, and Reed fell
into Dora's chair. He waved Katie into one of the other chairs in
the office, then rocked back. "Craig, Eric's medical records are
attached to the casefile. Update those. Thanks." Katie felt a
sudden, unexpected pang of doubt, but as soon as Reed pulled up
the medical records it was gone. Theresa had been true to her
word. When she'd checked out the casefile back in DC, the
medical records had been sparse, including a chart transcription
from when he was eighteen and regular updates throughout his
college years, but nothing since then.

Now it overflowed, rich with the hidden Hippocrates data
from the last decade. His monitored vitals updated in real-time,
but Katie and Reed were both far more interested in his past.
Reed skipped back to the day of the accident, and Katie
immediately jumped up out of her chair to slam a finger down on
the display.

"There!" she said, pointing to a red alarm in the data stream.
"He spiked. Oh, man. Look at those numbers. He was poisoned,
right here! Why didn't Hippocrates respond?"

"False alarm," Reed said, pointing to the cancellation two lines
down. "The watches aren't perfect, and we can't afford to send

emergency response teams out to fix a malfunctioning watch, so if vitals recover within a certain amount of time—"

"Yes, but how could someone take advantage of that? If there were a poison that did that, I'm sure Hippocrates would monitor for it, right?"

Reed shook his head. "Nope. It's just like Dora said. Someone used the clinic to engineer the perfect drug for him."

Katie shook her head. "I asked the research assistant about the chief's theory of the crime, and she said their technology doesn't work like that. Whatever this is, it'd have to be something that already existed, and something that did *exactly* this. Where would someone find something like that?"

His vitals were normal after the all-clear, for hours. It wasn't until his blood sugar dipped late in the night that Hippocrates took any note of him again, and a day later he was on machines flooding the record with extra information. "That whole time," she said. "That pushes our timetable back almost ten hours. Reed, that false alarm was the incident. He crashed, fell into a coma, and normalized within five seconds." She shook her head, horrified.

"What did his doctors have to say about it?" Reed asked, and then set to finding his own answer.

He pulled up the army's medical analysis, but it was blank. "This document is unavailable for reasons of national security."

"Nuh uh," Reed said. "That doesn't cut it. Hathor, connect me to Lieutenant Drake. Thanks."

"He's not going to help you," Katie said. She closed out the restricted document and started looking for something else—a summary, an official opinion, anything to show the army's investigators had caught the false alarm.

"Drake, this is Agent Reed," he said, and Katie could tell by the tone of his voice he was leaving a message. And he wasn't happy. "We have official permission to access Eric Barnes's medical records, and, dammit, I've got clearance higher than you do, so I demand access to your medical report. Hippocrates is showing it as sealed. Get back to me. Goodbye. *Damn*!"

"It's okay," Katie said, trying to calm him. "We'll get it sorted out." Her eyes were locked on the desktop, scanning rapidly. "They pulled bloodwork...there." She pointed to a flurry of activity in his medical record. "This has got to be the army investigation. We can't see their results, but can we access their samples?"

"Depends how they ran them," Reed said. "Craig, connect me to Dimms. Dimms, hi, it's Reed. I need you to find out anything you can about Barnes's medical exam. Katie thinks she's spotted the time of his attack, and we've found where the army ran some tests, but they're locking us out of the test results. Can you do anything with that?" He waited, listening, then said, "Sure, yeah. Just a sec." He scrolled back up through the medical history and tapped on the desktop, adding a comment to the false alarm. Then he went back and did the same to the blood samples Katie had spotted. "There," he said. "Should be up now."

A moment later he nodded. "Let us know. This could be crucial. Thanks, Dimms. Goodbye." He turned to Katie. "That's good work. It'll take him some time to figure it out, because medical simulations take a while, but—oh. Hmm." He held up a finger again. "Yeah, connect me. Hey, Dimms, hold up. Craig, connect us to Katie. Thanks." Katie quickly accepted the call, and Reed said, "Go ahead. Problems with the simulation?"

"What? Oh, no. No. It's done."

Reed frowned. "You're kidding."

"Not at all. Tox screens can take a long time because they're looking for so many different things, many of which express themselves in subtle ways after they've been metabolized." He paused, and Katie could hear him working. "Yeah," he said. "Just double-checked it, and the numbers are right. See, I thought I'd rule out the most obvious first, before running the general screen, but it came up positive. Majorly. Your boy was drugged."

Katie and Reed exchanged glances. "That...I mean, that's sort of the theory we were working on..." she said.

"It's nasty stuff," Dimms said. "Something Barnes was working on back in college, actually. It was supposed to be an anaesthetic, but it was unsuccessful in human studies—"

"Unsuccessful how?" Reed asked.

"You're looking at it," Dimms said. "Worked in rats, worked in sims, but they didn't have comprehensive simulations back then. Turns out it doesn't work in people. It went to clinical trials and put five patients into comas before they figured that out."

It took Katie a moment to find her voice. Her mind kept jumping back to her visit to Theresa Barnes, the woman's desperate devotion. She said softly, "What's the recovery like?"

"There's not one," Dimms said. "It's been years, and none of them has come around. Three died in the hospital from complications of their initial maladies, one was taken off a feeding tube two years ago and...allowed to die. And...the other one is still completely unresponsive."

"Get us their records, attach them to the casefile," Reed said, but Dimms cut him off.

"Can't. They're restricted. US Army."

Katie's breath escaped her. "So they know."

"Yeah," Reed said. "Yeah, fast as we found this, they would have to know."

Katie's eye widened. "They're covering for her?" She jumped to her feet, her heart racing. "They know about this and they're covering it up?"

As if in answer the office door swung open, and all eyes went to it. Lieutenant Drake stood framed in the doorway. "No," he said simply, considering the two agents with tired eyes. "We're hunting her down."

12. Manhunt

The lieutenant was carrying a file folder, which he tossed down casually on the desktop. He spoke to Reed. "I was coming to give you that. It's our only copy of the medical report. We pulled the digital one when we discovered the significance of it."

Reed held the lieutenant's eyes for a moment, then he sighed. "Dimms, we're going to have to call you back. Keep me posted on the TMS analysis, though. Goodbye." He flipped open the folder and scanned the top page. He didn't look up when he asked the lieutenant, "What did you find?"

"We found evidence Barnes was poisoned. The chemical agent that induced his coma is a severely restricted compound. It's water soluble and nearly tasteless, so it would have been easy enough to administer if you weren't exremely concerned with the dosage." Drake stepped into the room and closed the door behind him. "Apparently your men knew what to look for. Ours didn't, so it took some time to track it down."

"Why didn't you tell me?" Reed said. He still didn't look up, and Katie could see his knuckles were white. His jaw clenched.

Drake caught it, too. His tone was respectful, friendly. "We wanted to take care of it ourselves. There were signs pointing to Ellie from the first—"

"Like what?" Reed demanded. He looked up, and there was a ferocity in his eyes. "What did you know?"

Katie was impressed that the lieutenant didn't look away. He said, "I'm not at liberty to say."

"Where is she?"

The lieutenant shrugged. "Your guess is as good as mine." He chuckled. "Maybe better."

"Probably." Reed nodded. "You should have told us. You're playing games here—"

"We are *not* playing games," Drake said, suddenly cold. "We are acting as faithful stewards of state secrets, Mister Reed. It is a difficult burden—"

"And you shut us out," Reed said. He shook his head. "We're Ghost Targets. This is what we *do*, lieutenant. You could have saved us hours of work if you'd just told us this morning. You could have put it in your report—"

"No." He sighed, and glanced at Katie. "Does she have to be here?"

A sarcastic smile tugged at the corner of Reed's mouth. "She knows more than I do." He leaned back in the chief's chair. "Yes, she does have to be here. We've both got clearance. Spill it."

The lieutenant leaned back against the door and crossed his arms over his chest. "Ellie Cohn somewhere in town," he said. "We know that much. She was at the clinic yesterday and none of our people were there to catch her, but we were able to stick her with a crippled car."

"Bugged?"

He shook his head. "We take our privacy measures very seriously, Agent Reed. The private taxis are all clean, and we would have tipped our hand if we'd given her anything else."

"You didn't have to give her anything at all," Katie said.

The lieutenant only looked annoyed. "We are *not* Ghost Targets," he said, and then he shook his head. "She wasn't acting skittish. Until yesterday she was on a normal routine, and we wanted to keep her handy until we knew what we were dealing with."

Reed chuckled. "You were trying to draw her out."

"This is not about a broken heart, Agent Reed." He hesitated, measuring, and Katie wondered just how much he was going to tell. He said, "This woman was looking to sell state secrets to foreign nationals. We're confident of it, but we don't have any proof."

"And you were watching her to get some," Reed said. "Or to catch the buyer."

"Chucking her in the brig for what she'd done to Eric wouldn't have brought the poor bastard back," Drake said. "We needed to fix the bigger problem."

"We could have helped," Reed said.

Drake shrugged. "Our entire goal was to keep the secret safe. Sharing it with an outside agency seemed counterproductive."

"And yet here you are."

Drake's lips tightened in a smile. "You have proven resourceful," he said, then he sighed. "And so has Ellie. She's gone to ground, and there's nothing we can do to find her."

For a long time Reed said nothing. Then he rolled his eyes and leaned forward to clear out the medical report on the desktop and replace it with a full-screen rendering of the TMS analysis. The solid yellow line of Ellie's likely path had grown half a mile longer since they'd checked it in the car, but it had also split in two, snaking in different directions from the next intersection.

Drake's eyes widened. "Is that her?"

"It's a probability analysis based on inconsistencies in the Traffic Management System record," Reed said. "We have her leaving the clinic yesterday a little bit after two." Drake nodded offhand, and Reed considered him for a moment. "Is that right?'

"That's right," Drake said. "One of our techs was in the garage when she requested a car, and he alerted me. She was gone by the time I got there."

"Well, we're trying to track where she went. Your tech's little stunt makes our job a lot easier, because we know she can't have gone too far."

The lieutenant stepped up to the desk and spent some time studying it. Then he reached out to trace the perimeter with a finger. "Somewhere in here," he said, shaking his head. "But her apartment is here." He jabbed a thumb down on the map northeast of the clinic, well outside the projected path. "She was already on the run, then. We've had people scouring the wrong part of town."

"Now's the time to fix that," Reed said. "Get your men out west. I have Chief Hart's people knocking on doors, and US Marshals on the way." He saw the concern in Drake's eyes and shook his head. "Your sting is over, Lieutenant. Let it go. Right now our only priority can be catching this woman."

After a moment Drake nodded. "Of course," he said. "I'll pass the order." He stepped out of the office and pulled the door closed behind him as he started giving commands over his headset.

Reed looked from the closed door to Katie. She still stood on the other side of the desk. He dropped his voice nearly to a whisper. "What do you think?"

"I think he knows he made a mistake, or you would not have survived telling him off like that." He looked offended and she laughed. "I'm sorry, sir, but I think he could take you."

He shook his head. "You think we can trust him, though?"

Katie bit her lip. She shook her head. "I think we're both after the same thing right now. That's not exactly the same as trust, but it's good enough."

Reed nodded. "Then we need to get back to work." He brought up a list of datapoints on the desktop, each one mapped to a spot within the broad avenues of Ellie's likely trajectory, and said, "She had to stop at some point. Most of the plots in the the TMS analysis captured gaps in high-speed traffic, but there are a handful that represent entrances and exits. We can check audio sources at these places and times to try to find out what Ellie did once she abandoned the car."

"How?" Katie said with a frown. "Do we stake out those spots in HaRRE?"

Reed shook his head. "Wouldn't do any good. HaRRE only shows positive IDs. We're working low-confidence audio here." He opened another tab on the casefile, which showed a list of audio files. "These, to be specific. They generally match the times and locations of the traffic deviation events, and have voiceprints with a base confidence between five and fifty for Ellie."

"That's quite a range," Katie said.

"It's garbage," Reed said. "Most of it is just noise. But we start at the top, highest confidence, and work our way down. If we can find just one more definite location, it could easily collapse her location to something we could use." He divided the audio files into two batches and assigned half of them to Katie. "You work those, I'll work these. See what you can find."

She went back to her chair and settled into it while the first audio clip played. It was marked as forty-seven percent base confidence, but all she heard over her headset was a brief yelp. It was a fraction of a second, and then it was over. She had Hathor generate the audio surrounding the clip, but there was nothing useful in the context. It could have been an audio glitch as easily as a person's voice, and there was certainly no way to identify it.

She shook her head and moved on to the next file, which included a woman's voice in a brief gap in otherwise overwhelming traffic noise. The words "get there" were obviously in the middle of a sentence, and accented such that she couldn't possibly identify it. She brought up HaRRE then to see what was going on, and found a likely source of the audio clip in a woman walking down the sidewalk talking to a ghost. The woman with the positive ID was a local resident who worked for a bakery nearby, though. Nothing sinister there, and no connection to Ellie Cohn.

Katie wasted five minutes following the pair until they wandered in range of a video camera, and when Katie switched to source video she got a clear view of the speaker. Definitely *not* Ellie Cohn—ten years too old and two inches too short.

Reed didn't seem to be having much more luck. Katie was trying her hardest to recognize the words or the voice behind a ten-second whisper at thirty-three percent confidence when Reed suddenly jumped to his feet, threw his handheld down on the desk, and stormed out of the office in frustration. She turned to find him talking with Drake outside, but it didn't look like a confrontation. He'd probably just needed a break.

Katie felt the need for one, too, but she fought it down. She closed out the unintelligible whisper, and then opened up the next file in the list. It was an old man in a convenience store, chatting with a young woman who Katie would guess was an employee. The girl's voice was nothing at all like Ellie's, and Katie was about to close out this file, too, when she clearly heard Ellie's voice in the background. "Just the coffee. Thanks."

Katie's eyes shot wide, and she skipped back to make sure she'd heard it right. The voice was quiet, and the old man spoke over her on "coffee," but Katie felt certain. She pounded a hand on the office window then leaned forward over the desk to find the file. She played it as Reed and Drake entered the office, and the old man's flirtations blasted out of the desktop's speakers. Katie left the volume high.

Reed frowned, listening, and he had the same reaction she had, shaking his head when the girl spoke, but a moment later Ellie spoke into the room and Reed and Drake both gaped. Katie grinned. "That's Ellie."

"That is," Reed said. He hurried around the desk to get the details on the audio clip, and then he grinned. "That's square in the southwest corridor, Katie. Craig, connect me to Dimms. Thanks. Dimms! Katie found us another match. Plug this in." He looked at Drake. "She was at the store at two thirty yesterday afternoon. Get one of your men there to interview the employees. I'll pull surveillance footage within a half-mile radius for the next half hour, and grab identities on any other customers in the store, just in case. What?" He stopped, listening to something from Dimms, and nodded. "I'm not surprised. Put it up."

He cleared out the file list so they could see the TMS analysis full-screen again, and now there was no circle, but a much narrower, much brighter corridor stretching south and west from the earlier line. "That's great, Dimms. Thanks. Yeah. Goodbye." He pointed to the map, aglow with victory. "That's maybe twelve square miles. It's not going to be easy, but we can find her in that."

"Well," Katie said, "we can find where she was yesterday, sometime around three o'clock."

"The car's dead," Reed said, "and if she'd gotten access to another one, we would have spotted it by now. Unless you've got truly remarkable resources on your side," he said, with a significant look to her, "transportation is pretty much ghost-proof."

Katie remembered her own time ghosted, running from the authorities with Martin. The memory brought something else to mind. "What about her watch?" Katie said. "We've got Hippocrates data on Barnes from within the clinic. Did they all have special watches?"

"Yes," Drake said, narrowing his eyes. "How did you know?"

She smiled. "I know the man who invented them. Where's the server?"

He shook his head. "I don't understand."

"Those watches don't use the Hippocrates server. That's how they preserve the wearers' privacy. You had to set up a little local server, and they all sync to it. When something happens, the watches can trigger an event that transfers the local records into Hippocrates."

"Yeah," Drake nodded. "That's how it works, but we don't have a local server. The guy who set it up took care of that."

Reed looked to Katie. "Martin?"

"That's it," the lieutenant said. "Martin Door. That was before my time, though."

Katie nodded. Reed still held her gaze, and she realized he was trying to ask her something without words. If she could get in touch with Martin, if he had access to the server, he could get an exact location on Ellie from her watch. Reed didn't know Martin was already doing eveything he could to track her down, though. Katie shook her head, ever so slightly, and then winced at the look of disappointment in Reed's eyes.

"Not that, then," he said. "It was a good thought, though."

"I'll follow it up," she said. "I just—"

"Yeah," Reed said. "Look, the TMS analysis is still running. We'll get our searchers out on the streets looking for her, but that program is going to continue to refine things. If we can find the car, chances are good she's there, or within a one-day walk of there." He nodded, getting his steam back. "And we can narrow *that* down by places she could get unseen and unheard. The car actively concealed her identity within a short range, but if she just climbed out of it and started walking back into town, Hathor would have had an ID on her within minutes."

"Unless she concealed it," Drake said.

"No," Reed said. "You filled me in on everything she can do. Remember, these are the tools of my trade. She can do some amazing work after the fact, but she can't ghost herself on the fly."

"What if someone's working with her?" Katie said, still thinking of her time with Martin. She caught Reed's eye. "What if it's somebody special?"

He frowned, then turned to the lieutenant. "What do we know about her buyers?"

"Nothing," Drake said, bitter. "We've got nothing on them, and that's a frightening prospect. I was hoping you two had come up with something—"

Katie shook her head. Reed answered more accusingly, "We were late to that party," he said. "We only just found out about it."

Then a thought struck Katie, and she spoke up. "What about the recording?" Both men turned to her, and she nodded enthusiastically. "The recording from Theresa. Remember? We have Eric ending his relationship with Ellie."

Reed looked blank, but Drake understood. He narrowed his eyes suspiciously at her. "We don't want anyone to know this." He pointed a threatening finger at Reed. "We don't want *anyone* to know this, but we have some suspicions that Eric could be an accomplice in her plans."

Katie nodded. "I think we're getting our information from the same source," she said. "If their relationship was something other than romantic, then we might find something useful in the breakup."

Drake looked across to Reed. "Have you watched it yet?"

"It's just audio," Katie said. "And no, he hasn't. It was just me, and that was before I had any idea. Hathor, play the Snoopy audio file on this desk. Thanks."

It started with Ellie's voice, that gentle purr promising him whatever he wanted, and Katie cringed again. Her new understanding didn't make it any better. Drake looked just as unhappy, hearing his soldier openly seducing the good doctor. He shook his head when Eric first told her no.

"What was she doing before he showed up? That could be more useful than his sudden change of heart. Go back."

"There's no back," Katie said. "Ellie cleared this whole conversation out of the archive. I only have this snippet because Mrs. Barnes had hired a service to make sure Eric wasn't trying to leave her."

"So it's a copy?" He hung his head. "We can't even get location information out of it?"

"We may be able to get some," Reed said, while Ellie screamed her objection over the speakers. "There's some ambient noise that we might be able to isolate. You can hear a voice through a window or wall at three seconds. It's muffled, but we may be able to get something."

"I have a better idea," Katie said, rising from her position in the corner. "If you would excuse me...." She left the office and pulled the door closed. Then she said, "Hathor, connect me to Meg Ginney. Thanks."

Katie didn't expect an answer. It was after five by then, but the girl could easily still be at the clinic. She answered on the third ring, though. "Hello?"

"Meg, I've got a question for you and I need you to answer me honestly."

"Wh—what?" She stammered, surprised by Katie's tone, but Katie didn't have time to soothe her.

"You said you and Eric almost got together," she said. "Would it have been at the clinic?"

"I...Miss Pratt, I really don't want to talk about that."

Katie sighed. "This is important, Meg."

"No," she said. "No, all he could think about was work at the clinic. It would have been somewhere else." She sounded bitter at having to answer, but Katie couldn't let it go.

"Where then?" Katie said. "I know you said nothing happened, but if you can think of anything, if you know anything at all—"

"Okay," Meg said, shouting. "There was a motel. Okay? We only went there once, and we didn't end up doing anything—"

"But where?" Katie said, excited. "Where was it?"

"The Sunrise Inn." The girl took a deep breath, and let it out. "I don't know where it is. Okay? Is that all?"

"That's all," Katie said. "Thank you for your help." Before she could say more, Meg cut the connection. Katie had what she wanted. She burst back through the office door, triumphant, and said, "Craig, show location details for the Sunrise Inn on Dora's desk." A glowing marker appeared, just west of center in the TMS analysis projection path, and Katie smiled. "She's there," she said. "She's at the Inn."

13. At the Sunrise Inn

"Where'd you pull that out of?" Reed said, but Katie waved the question away.

"Bring up the security footage for the place. Even if her ID is hidden, I bet you can get a good look at her face." She looked at the map and guessed at the distance from the convenience store to the motel. "Start at two fifty, but I'm guessing she got there around three oh five."

Reed nodded and pulled up video source from the motel's parking lot. Lieutenant Drake was still curious, though. "How did you find that place?"

"Barnes had used it for his romantic trysts before," Katie said. "She would have been comfortable there. Stands to reason if she were laying low, but had a reason to stay in town, she'd go somewhere familiar."

"Somewhere she knows how to hide from Hathor." Drake nodded. "That's good thinking."

"That's her," Reed said, and the other two turned to find a still frame of Ellie Cohn, frozen as she climbed out of her private taxi.

"What room is that?" Katie said, leaning closer. Pull up a floor plan of the hotel."

"No," Reed said, jumping to his feet. "Craig, save all that to the casefile and push it to my handheld, then clear out the desk. Thanks." He was already across the room, open door in his hand. "Come on," he said. "We're going to make this bust."

Katie caught up with him in the hall, Drake a step behind her. Reed was talking into his headset. "Dora, we've found her. I'm sending you location information now. Can you assign one of your cars to bring Katie and me out there? Thanks."

"That's not necessary," Drake said. "I have a car—"

"And you're going to need it to bring Ellie back to the base," Reed said. "We'll ride separate. See you at the Inn." With that he pushed the outer door open and held it for Drake. The lieutenant had no choice but to step out into the sunlight, where his car still waited by the door.

A moment later Katie and Reed followed after him as one of the police cars pulled up to the curb. Katie quipped, "Hoping for another private conversation?"

Reed answered deadpan. "Yes," he said as he pulled his door closed. "I was hoping you could contact Martin for me."

"I...." Katie's smile faded. "That's not how it works."

"That *is* how it works," Reed said, "and you've been holding out on me."

"I don't just call Martin. He doesn't answer—"

"I don't believe that," Reed said. "I've seen you two together, don't forget that."

"Please, Reed, you've got to believe me—"

Martin spoke in her ear. "It's okay," he said. "Find out what he wants."

Reed spoke almost in answer to him. "I want to know who Ellie was dealing with, and exactly what information she was trying to sell them. If we can't get those, Drake's cooperation ends as soon as Ellie is in his custody."

"I can do the first part," Martin said. He sounded agitated. "But I have no intention of telling him what Ellie knows. Katie, I'm serious—"

"Don't worry about that," Katie said soothingly, then to Reed's questioning look. "I'll try to get it done."

"Good," Reed said, settling back with his handheld. "I'm going to start putting our case in Jurisprudence. Now we know it's a poisoning, we can get things moving."

For Reed's sake, Katie pretended to record a voice note to Martin, but Martin was already off the line working on Reed's search. After she passed on the request, Katie pulled out her own handheld and started reviewing the security footage of Ellie. She showed up at the hotel stumbling, looking tired in spite of the coffee she'd picked up down the road.

"Hmm," Katie said, and after a moment Reed looked up.

"What?"

"Why...." Katie tapped her handheld and switched to the convenience store video. "Why would she stop for a coffee, if she was on the run?"

"Did you see her at the motel? That girl was dead on her feet. Probably needed the caffeine just to make it to her bed." He shook his head. "I'm guessing she hasn't slept for days."

"But why stop somewhere public?" Katie watched the short video loop through twice. Ellie definitely looked like she was dragging, swaying on her feet while she filled her coffee cup. "She had to leave traffic, which automatically added ten minutes to her drive, then go into a crowded shop just to get some cheap black coffee when she could have made up a pot in the privacy of her hotel room."

"Habit," Reed said. "I checked while you were on the phone. Ellie's been to that convenience store before. On the day of Theresa's recording, for one."

"Whenever she goes out to the motel, then."

"Probably so." He shrugged. "People make stupid mistakes. It's the only reason we can do our jobs."

"Well, that and the assistance of the terrible Martin," Katie said. It earned her a black look from Reed, but she ignored it and went back to her examination of the Sunrise Inn.

Ellie's car was parked at the north end of the west parking lot, hidden from view of the road. That also put her in one of the rooms from eighteen to thirty-six, on either floor. Katie pulled up the registry and quickly eliminated half of the rooms by their occupants. Then she started checking through security feeds for the empty rooms. She didn't see Ellie in any of them, but the feed from room one twenty-one was blank.

"I might have something," she said. She did a search through the archives, but couldn't find a record of anyone renting that room in recent history. She tried to book it but the motel's reservation service told her it was unavailable, now, next week, and next year. "Yeah," she said to Reed. "I think she's in one twenty-one."

"Good," he said. "Dora has three teams there now." He passed the information along to the police, ending it with, "Be careful."

Katie frowned. "You think she's dangerous?"

"I think she's a powerful person, uniquely skilled, and backed into a corner," he said. "That is always dangerous."

Katie looked back down at her handheld, which showed a view of the parking lot, Ellie's car close to the camera, and nothing moving. "What is she up to?"

While she was still trying to guess, Reed started receiving video feed from Dora at the motel. He shared it to Katie's handheld and she opened it up, curious. When Reed noticed, he connected her to his audio link with the Chief, too.

The recorder in Hart's car had a much better angle on room one twenty-one. The covered walk that gave access to the second floor rooms acted as an overhang for the first floor, and the door to Ellie's room sat way back in the shadows of that overhang. The only window into the room was tall and narrow, six feet to the right of the door. The blinds were drawn, of course.

Hart's car was in the parking lot just behind Ellie's, with two other police cars to the right and left, forming a barricade around the room. Katie watched as one of the officers approached to knock on the door, but he got no response. Most of the rooms next to Ellie's were empty, but Katie saw officers go to the one above her and the one next to that to speak with the inhabitants. The cop by Ellie's door tried one more time, then withdrew as someone off-camera started calling out to Ellie over a bullhorn.

Dora said softly, "I hope you know what you're talking about, Reed." She was standing just in front of the camera, off to the right, facing away toward the motel. She shook her head, and said, "Is she even in there?"

"We've got her on camera entering the place," Katie said, "and she never left. She's in there."

For a moment, Hart said nothing. Then she looked back over her shoulder, a glance at the camera, and she sighed. "Is she dangerous?"

Katie looked to Reed, expecting him to give his trapped animal speech again, but instead he said, "Hathor, connect us to Lieutenant Drake." He waited for the connection, then said, "Drake, we've got men on the scene—"

"I'll be there in five," Drake said, sounding satisfied.

"We need to know what to expect," Reed said, as though he hadn't been interrupted. "Is Ellie armed?"

"Should be, yeah." The lieutenant thought for a moment, and said, "Yeah, she'll have her sidearm on her. Can't see her carrying anything heavier than that."

Reed said, "I don't suppose it's got an identity lock on it?"

Drake chuckled. "Wouldn't do much good in her line of work, would it?"

"I suppose not." Reed sighed. "Did you get that, Dora?"

"Suspect is armed. Got it. I'll pass the word, but we were operating under the assumption, anyway."

"She's not just armed," Drake said, his voice gruff. "I've seen that girl on the firing range. She's deadly. You should probably wait for me to get there—"

Hart bristled. "My men can handle this, Lieutenant."

"I'm sure they can, but I need Corporal Cohn alive. You just sit tight. I'm already on my way—"

"With all due respect, you don't have any jurisdiction here, so how about you keep your advice to yourself?"

Katie looked to Reed again, but he was helpless to stop the catfight that was emerging between the other two. Katie just rolled her eyes and dropped out of the connection. "Tell me if they say anything important," she said, and went back to the surveillance footage at the convenience store. She watched it play through, zoomed in close, looking for some clue to what was going on behind Ellie's tired eyes. "Why were you there?"

Reed leaned across to see what Katie was looking at, and his eyes narrowed. "You could be on to something," he said. He pulled up the casefile on his own handheld, and shook his head. "God, I should have listened to you. Katie, what if she met her buyer there?" Katie frowned, considering, but Reed went on. "That could explain her exhaustion, if she'd been trying to move things ahead of schedule. Could explain what's going on now, too. She's sleeping off three days of pure anxiety."

Katie could understand that. Of course, she'd been under anesthetic and on severe painkillers after her experience with Martin, but even without that—without the injuries—she knew she would have been useless for days after getting home. She considered Reed for a moment, who had tried so hard to convince her to stay home for another week. His eyes were locked on his handheld, as he scoured the same short video footage Katie had been looking at for the last ten minutes, looking for some sign of their culprit. She smiled at him anyway.

He looked up and caught just the edge of her smile, which made him cock his head in curiosity. He didn't ask, though, too busy with other matters. "We've got a list of positive IDs for everyone in the store with her, right? Have you checked that against video source?" Katie shook her head, and he nodded. "Okay. We need to do that, to see if there's any other ghosts there with her." He cleared out the video playback and made a note to himself, then pulled up Ellie's personal information. "I wish we had more here." There were three tabs, all of them scant on information. He opened up the empty medical history, and Katie's eyes widened.

"Martin!" She said, then shook her head. "Hathor, connect me to Martin. Thanks." Hathor gave her nothing, and Katie sighed. "Martin, I need your help." Reed watched Katie, interested.

Martin answered her a moment later, a little breathless. "What's up?"

"Get us Ellie's medical history. It's on a private Hippocrates server, right? Just like yours?"

"Katie!" Martin sounded scandalized, and Katie just laughed.

"Reed knows, Martin. You tipped your hand at Velez's."

"*You* tipped my hand," Martin said, then sighed. "And it probably saved our lives. Okay, yeah, I helped set up something like it for the clinic—"

Katie leaned forward. "Can you dump Ellie's records into the system?"

"I...yeah. Yeah, I can do that," Martin said. "Give me a moment."

Katie watched Reed's handheld until Martin said, "There. Done." A moment later the screen updated, with a long scroll of medical history previously obscured. "I hope there's nothing in there too revealing," Martin said, and Katie knew exactly what he meant.

"I can't see how there would be," Katie said. "But I'll take care of it if there is."

Martin laughed darkly. "Is that all?"

Katie didn't answer right away. She had the medical history open on her own handheld, scanning through it at the same time Reed was, looking for the fatigue Reed was so sure of. She spoke without looking up. "What are we looking for, Reed?"

"Find the signs of her anxiety," he said. "Figure out where it started, where it spiked, and maybe we can find a hidden call to her buyer. I just don't see...."

Katie didn't see it either. There was nothing over the weekend to reflect the exhaustion Ellie showed so clearly on the tape. A quick analysis of her breathing and heart rate patterns showed a regular sleep schedule, too, right up until yesterday morning. Reed's prediction bore out her crash, though. From the look of it, she'd been sound asleep in the hotel room ever since she'd gotten there yesterday afternoon. Katie pointed it out to Reed, and he immediately got back on the line with the police chief.

"Dora," he said. "We've got Ellie's vitals. She's in the hotel room all right, and it looks like she's asleep. If you can get your men in quickly—"

"Reed," Katie said, but he waved her away. She caught his arm with a surprising strength, and he turned to her. Her eyes blazed. "Reed," she hissed. "She's not asleep."

"What?"

The car slammed to a stop, and Katie looked up in surprise to see through the windshield the same scene she'd gotten from Hart's dash cam. They were there. Katie shook her head. "She's not asleep, Reed. She's in a coma."

He frowned, and she showed him her handheld. Just after she'd shown up yesterday, seconds after she'd been caught on camera stumbling from her car to the motel room door, Ellie's vitals had spiked. Six seconds later, door closed behind her, she'd fallen back into regular rhythms, and Hippocrates had marked the anomaly a false alarm.

It showed in four short lines on Ellie's medical history, but Katie knew how to interpret it because she'd seen it before. Reed recognized it, too. "What...how?" he said. "What does this mean?"

Katie froze at the question. Her mind raced, though, furiously putting the pieces together, rearranging them, trying them in other ways. For a moment she couldn't answer him, then Martin spoke in her ear. "What's happening?"

Something about his voice made it fall into place. In a flash she understood, and with that came a deep pit of fear in her stomach. She didn't let it show in her eyes.

"What it means," she said to Reed, perfectly cool, "is that you need to get out of the car."

He frowned. "I don't understand."

"And I don't have time to explain," Katie said, leaning across him to push his door open. Still close, noses almost touching, she breathed, "Please, Reed. Just trust me."

She could see in his eyes how much he disliked it. His jaw clenched. Outside, the lieutenant's car crunched to a stop on the asphalt beside them. At the same time Hart barked the order. "Go! Go! Go!"

"Katie..." Reed said quietly, pleading with her.

"Go," she said. "They're going to need you to sort this out."

He searched her eyes for an explanation, and shook his head when he didn't find one. "Katie—"

"Trust me," she said earnestly, and he must have felt the force of her urgency, because he finally relented. He slipped away from her and stepped out of the car, still holding Katie's eyes.

"I don't know what you think is going on—" he said, but she didn't hear the rest of his speech. She grabbed the door handle and slammed it closed, then engaged the locks.

"Driver," she said sharply, "take me to the Barnes house. It's urgent. Thanks."

She saw the surprised look on Reed's face, in the instant before the car screamed out of the parking lot and back into traffic heading east. Hart and Drake both converged on him, apparently still feuding, but Katie knew that wouldn't distract him for long.

"Are you still there, Martin?"

"I'm here, Katie," he said, and she breathed a sigh of relief. He asked again, "What's happening?"

"It wasn't Ellie," she said. "Stop searching for her buyer. We have more pressing—"

"I'm done," he said simply, cutting her off.

She blinked. "Huh?"

"I found her buyers," he said. "They weren't nearly as careful as Miss Cohn. I just handed the necessary information off to the FBI."

"Wow," Katie said. "That's great, Martin!" It took her a moment to remember what she was doing, then a look like panic came across her face. "Martin! Can you lock out this car?"

"What?"

"I need you to take over this car *right now*! If Reed or Hart thinks to shut it down, Gevia's done."

He sounded doubtful. "I don't understand—"

"Do it!" Katie shouted. "I'll explain later." She checked the driver monitor, which said she had eight minutes to the destination at top speed. She could feel the car barreling along, weaving through traffic that created precision lanes for the emergency vehicle as it pushed toward a hundred and twenty miles per hour. She glanced out the window, and it still seemed too slow. She spat out a string of dark curses, then pulled up Theresa's personal details on her handheld.

Martin interrupted her. "Okay," he said. "I think that did it. I just restricted Hart's access on this vehicle, and cleared Reed out of it. You're still in control." He hesitated for just a second, then said with a little too much unconcern, "Why are you going to Eric's place?"

"Hold on a second, Martin," she said. "Hathor, connect me to Theresa Barnes, high priority. Thanks." She waited through two rings and left a quick message, then tried again. Still nothing. Katie pounded a fist against the window. "Why isn't she answering?"

"She doesn't have her headset," Martin said.

"What do you mean?"

"Look at her location history," Martin said. "It stopped a while back. That means she doesn't have her headset or handheld—"

"Or her watch," Katie said. "Hathor, show me HaRRE. Thanks." Still several minutes away from the house, she pulled it up on her handheld and started searching. She checked throughout it, praying she was worrying over nothing, but the virtual house was completely empty.

"What time does the location history end?" she asked, too busy to check it herself.

Martin answered immediately, "Twenty minutes ago, give or take." Katie suspected he was doing the same thing she was.

She skipped the recreation backward twenty minutes and still found the house empty, but in the living room she found the front door standing open. She zipped out onto the porch and found Theresa there. She was dressed comfortably, light pants and a cotton shirt like she might have worn on a casual shopping trip. While Katie watched she closed and locked the door, humming some tune to herself, then turned back toward the front walk. Something caught her eye, and a smile blossomed across her face. "Oh, hi!" she said warmly. "If I'd known you were coming, I'd have baked a pie."

Katie checked, but the walk was empty, all the way to the curb. She knew what to expect, though. She watched Theresa's smile fade, then a moment later Meg Ginney materialized on the porch step within reach of Eric's wife. She had no smile for the older woman. Instead, she looked worried, hands clasped behind her back. "Mrs. Barnes," she said, "we have to go to the clinic right away."

"What's the matter?" Theresa said, concerned now.

"It's...it's Eric," Meg said, shifting nervously. She bounced on her toes. "I think something's wrong."

"Oh, nonsense," Theresa said with a relieved smile. "Eric is fine. I have a very expensive service monitoring his condition twenty-four, seven."

"Please, Mrs. Barnes," Meg said. "It's important."

Theresa shook her head, and her tone became maternal, almost condescending. "I'm sorry, Meg, I just don't have time right now." She took a step closer to the other woman, heading for the car that had just pulled up to the curb. "I do wish you'd called—"

"No!" Meg shouted, and shoved the older woman back, hard. Theresa lost her footing and went down, landing on her backside with a cry of pain. Meg gave a sob, too, which pulled Katie's worried gaze back to her.

The girl had a gun, comically oversized in her tiny hands, but the look on her face was dead serious. "Get up!" she screamed. "Get up! You're coming with me."

Theresa's calm was shattered. "Meg, Meg, what are you doing?" Her face crumpled.

"Stop it! Shut up!" Meg shouted. She made a grab for Theresa's arm but missed. She took a heavy step forward and the older woman cowered. Then Meg bent and grabbed her upper arm in a crushing grip, so she could pull the woman to her feet. She stepped back quickly, the gun still trained on Theresa. She snapped, "Stop crying! Take...take off your watch. Leave it here. The other stuff, too." When Theresa didn't respond, Meg battedthe headset off her ear. Then she stepped forward and ground it underfoot. The images of the women began to stutter, but the audio was still clear.

"You'd better listen to me," Meg said, trying to regain control of herself. Her voice was more level, but it had a manic edge to it. "I'm not messing around here. Do you believe me?" Theresa only whispered, and Meg said it louder. "Do you believe me?" She didn't wait for an answer this time, but pointed the gun at what must have been the courtesy recorder on the porch and fired it with a thundering boom. With the video source gone, the avatars of the two women froze instantly, puppets without masters.

A recorder somewhere in the house was still getting audio, though. Katie heard Theresa's scream at the gunshot, and then Meg's murderous threats. Theresa must have believed her by then, because Meg fell silent a moment later, and Theresa's wail began to dwindle. Then the sound was gone, and the motionless models winked out of existence, leaving Katie alone on the porch.

She realized she'd been holding her breath, and gasped for air. "Did you see that?" Her voice came out a scream, but she couldn't control it. "Martin, did you see that?" She glanced at the time in HaRRE and up at the clock on the driver's monitor. "Driver, get me to the De Grey Clinic! Now!"

14. Standoff

Martin said in wonder, "Where did she get a gun?"

"I don't know," Katie said, drawing her own gun and checking the clip. "But she's not afraid to use it. She didn't even flinch." Katie spotted the green light at the top of her pistol grip and she cursed. "I've got an identity lock on mine, Martin."

"Of course," Martin said. Then, "Oh."

Katie nodded. "I'm going to be unarmed as soon as I step onto the clinic grounds."

"Well, maybe she won't know," Martin said hopefully.

"Thinking like that is a good way to get shot," Katie said. She holstered her gun and checked the driver's monitor again. "Can you do something about it?"

"No." He sounded frustrated. "I had no part in that program."

"What about the clinic's security?" she said. "You set that up. Just turn it off."

"No, it's...I didn't...no." He laughed. "I didn't build the whole system, and most of it isn't stuff I can access remotely. The identity stuff specifically is all run locally."

"But you got the audio from my headset—"

"That's different," he said. "It's injected blind into the archive. Your gun requires a strong active ID, but the clinic is set up to hide IDs. Even if it had enough recorders to get the necessary overlapping coverage—which it doesn't—there are active isolation systems all over the campus. I can't just turn those off."

Katie sighed. "Well, maybe she won't know."

"Why are you going in at all?" he said. "Why did we lock out Reed and the local police? Get some backup—"

"For one," Katie said, "Theresa doesn't have the time." She fell back into her seat and let her eyes slip closed. "For another, Meg knows the secret."

"It's starting to seem like everyone knows the secret," Martin grumbled.

"Fewer and fewer," Katie said under her breath. She peeked at the monitor again, then took a slow, measured breath. "I need you to do something about those blind injections."

"What do you mean?"

"I'm two miles out, and I don't cherish the idea of charging in there alone. Find a way to activate my headset—"

"I can do that," he said. "It's an ugly workaround, but I made it happen before."

"Just be sure you can patch me through to Reed, too. But...I don't know, on a delay. Or with your hand on the button, anyway." She sighed. "Something."

"What are you talking about?"

"I'm talking about the secret," Katie said. "That's the motive here. Someone is thinning the list of people who can bring down Gevia."

"Meg."

Katie nodded. "Or...it could be Theresa." She shook her head. "I had thought maybe Theresa, but now it certainly looks like Meg."

"And you're going in there to—"

"To figure it out," Katie said. "To get a confession if I can, but to wrap this up without spreading the secret any further than it has to go." The car came to a stop at the curb, right behind one of the clinic's private taxis. Katie didn't see anyone through the window. "I'm doing this for you, Martin. I'm counting on you to keep me safe."

"I'll do what I can—"

"Good," she cut him off as she got out of the car. The sun was already setting behind the mountains, but its last angry red rays fell across the clinic's grounds to bathe the laboratory in a crimson glow.

Katie ran to the gate and stopped hard when it refused to open for her. "No!" She pounded a fist on the gate and shouted, "Dammit, no!"

"What?" Martin said.

"I don't have access rights now." Katie's eyes darted, searching the grounds beyond for any sign of movement, but there was none.

"I'm on it," Martin said, but Katie shook her head.

"There's no time for that. Hathor, connect me to Lieutenant Drake. Thanks."

Drake accepted her call, bringing her into a joint connection with Reed and Hart. Reed immediately said, "Katie! What are you doing?" He sounded afraid.

"I'm at the clinic," she said. "Meg Ginney abducted Theresa Barnes and brought her here at gunpoint." That drew gasps from all three.

"That would be Corporal Cohn's gun," Drake said. "That's why it's not on her."

"You hear that?" Reed said, a little frantic. "She's dangerous, Katie. You stay put. We're on our way—"

"No!" Katie said. "There's no time. Lieutenant, let me in."

"Absolutely not!" Reed said.

At the same time, the lieutenant stammered, "I'm not sure that's such a good idea. Clinic security can—"

Katie tuned him out when the gates suddenly swung open for her. She broke the connection and said, "God bless you, Martin."

"Their whole defense is based on anonymity," Martin said, fascinated. "This needs a complete redesign—"

"Not now," Katie said, charging the laboratory building. Lights were on inside, but she couldn't see anyone in the lobby. "Please tell me you got those doors open, too."

"For you, yes," he said. "But Meg Ginney isn't getting out."

She took a morbid comfort in that. One way or another, this ended here. "You're my hero," she said in a whisper and she pulled the door open and slipped into the lobby. "Now shut up."

She drew her sidearm as she crossed the room, padding lightly, eyes locked on the inner door. The three heavy bolts were open and the door open a crack. She could hear frantic voices on the other side of it. Her eyes flicked to her gun and she winced at the red light on its lock. Quietly as she could, she slipped into the next room.

Meg and Theresa stood close together at the far end of the room. The hospital curtains were thrown back from Eric's bed and the two women stood at his side, their backs to Katie. Meg was one step behind Theresa, the gun probably buried in the small of the older woman's back. Katie took her chance and slipped through the door, then darted to the nearest lab table and ducked behind it. Just then Theresa screamed, "No! No, please don't! I'm sorry."

Katie risked a look around the corner and saw Meg holding the older woman at arm's length now, with the gun right in her face. "No!" Theresa cried, falling to her knees. "Please, Meg. Please!"

Katie moved, letting Theresa's wails cover the sound of her approach. She darted from table to table, always out of sight, but there was a thirty-foot gap at the end of the room, open space between her and the other women. Katie stopped behind the last table, but a glimpse of Meg's eyes told her she was out of time.

Theresa saw it, too. Her screams reduced to a quiet, raw whimper. "Please, Meg." She couldn't meet the girl's eyes, instead staring at the floor. "I won't tell. I'll never tell."

"It's too late," Meg said, and Katie saw her jaw set.

She moved, then, throwing herself into a sprint. Something gave her away, though—the sound of her first step, or the surprise in Theresa's eyes. Whatever it was, Meg reacted instantly. She toppled Theresa backward with a rough shove then whirled, bringing the gun to bear on Katie. She took a shot and missed Katie wide to the right, then trained the gun on her torso and barked, "Stop!"

All of that in three steps, and Katie was still too far away to try anything. She skidded to a stop, her hands out to her sides. "It's okay, Meg," she said. "We can take care of this."

"We can," Meg said with a shaky grin. Her eyes darted, unfocused, and she nodded to Katie's useless gun. "Drop it."

Katie let the gun fall, then shrugged. "There," she said. She put her hands up, showing Meg her palms. "See? I want to work with you."

Meg shook her head with a wild laugh. "Oh, no," she said. "You and I...." She trailed off. Her gaze drifted back over her shoulder, to Eric's still form. "We don't work together."

Katie inched forward, but Meg caught the movement. Her head snapped back around and she shouted, "Stay right there!"

"I will," Katie said, her voice soothing. She backed up a step. "I want to help you."

Reed spoke softly in her ear. "That's good," he said. "Calm things down. Keep her talking. We'll be there in seven minutes." At least Martin had that working.

Meg wasn't going to be calmed, though. Katie could see it in her eyes. The girl was frantic, probably insane. She laughed again. "I'm glad you're here."

"Meg, no," Katie said, conscious of the headset recording their conversation. She was playing too many games at once. "You're doing good work here. Don't sacrifice that—"

"Don't talk to me like that!" Meg shouted. "You're just like that whore. She thought she could talk me down." She cackled, and her eyes went unconsciously to the gun in her hands. "She thought she could talk me down, but she was already gone."

Katie didn't need Reed's prompt. She took a cautious step closer, "Ellie, you mean?" Meg looked up, into Katie's eyes, and for a moment there was confusion there. Katie said, "You're talking about Ellie Cohn?"

Meg's lip curled in disgust. "I don't understand how Eric could even touch her. She's horrible—"

"And she's gone now," Katie said, and moved another step closer. Theresa was sprawled on the ground behind Meg, and Katie could see in her eyes that the traumatized woman was trying to find the nerve to jump her captor. It was too dangerous, though. She beckoned Meg a step closer, out of Theresa's grasp. "You took care of her," she said.

"I did," Meg nodded, and a demonic smile played across her face. "She came here to accuse me. She came here to threaten me, but she didn't know what I could do."

Katie shook her head, "I don't understand. Why did she come back?"

"She thought she'd figured it out. She thought I'd hurt Eric because I was jealous. Of her." She spit those words out in disgust. "She came back here to blackmail me. That's why. She showed up so sure of herself, trying to boss me around—"

"But you didn't put up with that," Katie said. "You poisoned her."

"It was easy."

Reed spoke in her ear, "Got her! That's enough for Jurisprudence, Katie." He was trying to encourage her, to give her strength, but Katie took his message another way.

Meg took another step closer, still crowing about her victory. "She noticed, though. She noticed something was wrong, and then she...she hit me." She smiled and turned her head, craning her neck so Katie could see the bruise behind her ear, a black thumbprint on her throat. "She tried to choke me, but I got away. She didn't expect me to fight." She laughed. "She thought she would be stronger."

Theresa was up on her knees, now, but her plans had melted away. "Why?" she cried. "Why would you do all this?"

Katie shook her head. That was exactly what she wanted hidden from Hathor. "Martin," she said sharply, ignoring the startled looks from the other two women. "Kill it. Now!" She heard the tone as her headset finally went offline.

Meg's eyes narrowed. She took another step closer, two and a half paces away now, and gestured with the gun toward Katie's headset. "Who are you talking to?"

"Old habit," Katie said. "Sorry. These don't work in here."

Meg shook her head. "You're doing something."

"What could I do?" Katie nodded meaningfully toward her weapon on the floor, then took a long sideways step away from it. She shook her head. "All I want to do is get all of us out of here alive."

One corner of Meg's mouth twitched up in a smile. "That's not going to happen," she said. "You know how the saying goes. Three people can keep a secret if two of them are dead."

Katie held up a finger, "Wait! Wait." She shook her head. "This isn't going to make it better, Meg. A shootout at the Gevia clinic? Federal agents dead? They can't cover that up. I have family—"

"I don't care about your family!"

"You should," Katie said with artificial calm. "You should, because my family is going to want to know what happened, and the Bureau is going to tell them. They don't know about Gevia. They don't know how important this place is, so they'll tell my family I was gunned down by a research assistant at the De Grey Clinic, and *that* will make the news."

"No," Meg said, and Katie nodded.

"You can't do this," she said. "If you kill us here, it's over. That won't protect the secret—that will end it." She nodded toward Theresa, cowering on the ground. "She promised you she's not going to tell." Meg glanced her way, and Theresa nodded frantically. Katie drew her attention back with a wave of her hand, "And I promised you the same thing." She held Meg's eye.

"*Without* a gun in my face, Meg. Without any suspicion of what you were willing to do, I made that promise. Because I believe."

"It's important!" Meg wailed, and Katie nodded enthusiastically.

"It's crucial," she said. "How many lives depend on the secret?"

"All of them," Meg said, her eyes wide. "It's not a number. It's everyone. We can't risk that. Not for...for some...some *whore*." Sadness crept into her eyes, and she glanced back at Eric again. "Not even for him."

Katie slipped a step closer. "You had to kill them—"

"No!" Meg rounded on her, and jammed the gun in her face. "I didn't kill him! He's still alive—"

Katie had heard the argument before, but she wasn't interested. Meg was close enough now. Katie swept her arm up and knocked the gun away before Meg pulled the trigger. The report deafened her, but the bullet went wide. Katie stepped forward as she continued the motion, trapping Meg's wrist against her side, and she shoved, twisting the girl away from her. Meg growled, an angry, animal sound, but Katie had both the other woman's wrists behind her back now, and with a sharp motion she knocked the gun out of her hands, then pressed down with her shoulder and pushed the girl to her knees.

"You're under arrest," Katie said. "For assault on Ellie Cohn and Eric Barnes."

"I had to do it," Meg said, her voice eerily calm. "I had no choice. I loved him, but he was going to give it away."

"He wasn't," Katie said sadly.

"He was," Meg insisted, sadness weighing down her eyes. "Because of that vile woman. They were going to sell the secrets to some stupid dictator who wouldn't know how to keep them safe. They were going to give it all up, so I had to stop them."

"You didn't," Katie said sadly. "I told you before, we have a recording of them at the Sunrise Inn. He told her no. He told her it was over." Meg wrenched an arm free with surprising strength, but instead of fighting she gave a miserable sob and clasped a hand to her chest, as she had done before. This time Katie understood why. She saw the delicate silver necklace around the woman's neck. Katie snapped the chain with a sharp flick of her wrist, and when she pulled it away it came with a heavy gold ring dangling from it. Eric's class ring. She recognized it from the Hathor footage. "He was never a threat," she said sadly. "He never would have risked Gevia."

Meg hung her head, the fight gone out of her. Katie let the ring slip free of the chain, then tossed it to Theresa who caught it with a terrified awe. She stared at it for a moment, and then the reality of it all finally sank in. "You really did it," she said quietly.

Meg nodded, mute.

Theresa stumbled to her feet and came over to them, a fire burning in her eyes. "You did this to him. On purpose." She looked back and forth between Katie and Meg, replaying their conversation in her head, and ended by shouting, "For nothing! You did this to him for nothing!" She slapped Meg with a vicious backhand, rocking her head back with the force of it. "How could you?"

Katie said quietly, "Mrs. Barnes—" but Meg spoke up in answer.

"I had to," she said. "I did it because I had to."

"For the secret," Theresa said with disgust. "For that goddamned secret." She turned away, to face Eric, and Katie saw her shoulders fall. Theresa stepped closer to him and said, "All of this for a lie."

"It's not a lie," Meg said quietly. "It's real."

"It's a sham," Theresa said, rounding on her, but her rage was short lived. She turned back to Eric and tenderly took his hand to replace the stolen ring. "It's a waste."

"It's life," Meg said. "For the first time in human history, we are free to live."

Theresa turned then, the sadness bitter in her eyes. She waved her arms to indicate the room they were in, Eric unconscious on the bed behind her. "Is that what you call this? Freedom?"

Meg hung her head again. "Not us," she said. "We're a sacrifice. But isn't it worth it? Two lives lost to save millions? Billions?"

"More than that," Theresa said. "More lives are sacrificed to this lie. Yours and mine—"

"But it works out," Meg said. "What price would be so high that you would make everyone you know, everyone you love, grow feeble and slow? What price would be so high you would willingly condemn a nation full of healthy, happy people to senility and death? Would you really choose something else—anything else—over the lives of every other person on Earth?" Theresa's chin went up stubbornly, but Meg said quietly, "Would Eric?"

That stopped her, and Theresa crumpled. Meg did, too. The strength went out of her and she collapsed against Katie's legs. "I only did what I had to do."

Katie considered them both for a moment, measuring, then her eyes went to the clock on the wall and she sighed. "Are we going to do this, then?"

Theresa looked up to meet her eyes, curious, and Katie said more strongly, "Are we going to keep the secret?" She held Theresa's eye and said, "It's up to you."

"We have to!" Meg wailed. "If you don't, it was all for nothing! How can you even ask—"

"Stop." Katie said sternly, hauling Meg to her feet. She tangled two fists in the girl's shirt and pulled her nose-to-nose. "You don't have a say in this," she growled. "You gave it up when you started poisoning people."

"I had to," Meg said. "You know that. You know what Ellie almost did."

"We stopped her," Katie said. She pushed Meg back against the wall, probably a little harder than necessary. "We found her buyers, Meg, and they're going to go to jail. We found where she went to hide, based on nothing but a suspicion. If you had come to us in the first place, we could have shut her down."

"I couldn't trust an outsider to understand," she said fiercely. "I still don't, for that matter." The fury still burned in her eyes. Katie shook her head.

"You just don't get it," she said. "I'd almost like to walk outside and tell the whole world what was going on here, just to hurt you." She glanced back to Theresa, and shook her head. "But I can't. Because you're right."

"But—"

"So here's what we're going to do," Katie said, cutting her off. Her eyes darted to the clock again, and she spoke quickly. "You're going to confess to murdering Ellie Cohn out of jealousy."

Meg's eyes grew wide. "No...."

Katie nodded. "Yes. And you're going to tell the police you brought Mrs. Barnes here to kill her, too, for the same reason. Because you were in love."

Tears slipped from Meg's eyes. "I can't," she said, but Katie had no pity for her.

"You will," she said. "Because if you don't, if we have to take this to trial, I stand ready to take you down. I have no sympathy for what you've done." She touched her headset. "But I have everything I need to send you away forever, Meg. And Gevia would die in the process."

Katie saw the war raging behind Meg's eyes, and after a moment the girl nodded—a single, desperate jerk of the head. "Okay," she gasped. "Okay. Yes. It's my sacrifice." She took a deep breath. "I'll do it."

"It's still not up to you," Katie said, and Meg turned terrified eyes to Theresa. Katie looked over, too, and after a moment Theresa nodded solemnly.

"It's the right thing to do," she said.

Just then the door at the other end of the lab burst open. Reed was the first one through it, with Hart's police officers flooding in behind him. Katie put her hands up and called out, "It's all right. Situation's under control." Then she stepped closer to Meg while the police crossed the room and said, "You're going away somewhere real quiet, for a very long time. We're the secret keepers now."

Reed rushed to Katie as she stepped back. He turned her to face him, and searched her eyes with concern in his. "What's going on?" he said. Chief Hart stepped up behind her to cuff the girl. "We had you on Hathor, somehow..." he trailed off, looking around, and then shook his head, "and then you were gone."

"Call it a miracle," Katie said. "You got what you needed, right?"

He nodded, and she smiled. "Good. How's Ellie?"

Reed shook his head, not meeting Katie's eyes, and she felt her stomach sink with dread. "That bad?"

"She's at the hospital now, but she's in bad shape. That place was wrecked."

"She went there to die," Katie said. The full force of that struck her, and she looked down. "She didn't go home. She didn't go to a hospital. She knew what to expect—she'd seen what happened to Barnes—and she went to that fleabag motel—"

"Where she'd been happy," Reed said quietly. "I talked to Drake. I reviewed footage of the two of them together. I think she found some comfort there."

Katie shook her head. "What a mess." She looked up and found Theresa watching them. A blush rose into her cheeks, but the other woman pretended she hadn't heard their conversation.

She came clumsily to Katie, a bit unsure, then flung her arms around Katie's neck and squeezed her in a tight hug. "Thank you," she whispered in her ear. "Thank you so much."

"Of course," Katie said. "I just did what I had to." The unintentional echo of Meg's words seemed to strike them both at the same time, and Theresa stepped away.

She smiled. "I'm amazed what you were able to accomplish, what you were able to uncover, with so little information. You...you saved my life." Katie shrugged, her blush back, and Theresa turned to Reed. "She deserves a promotion."

"She's a fine agent," Reed agreed. "I'm sorry, Mrs. Barnes, but could you excuse us for just a moment?"

"Of course," Theresa said. She withdrew to the corner, where she took Eric's hand and in a moment all her attention was on her husband.

Katie watched her, fascinated. "She knows," she said absently. "She knows about everything that happened, and yet...."

"She's in love, Katie. Simple as that." He shook his head. "How did you know?"

Katie glanced around, checking that none of the police officers was close enough to overhear, then she leaned forward with a shrug. "It was Martin," she said quietly. "You knew all along. Without him, we could not have finished this investigation."

He held her eyes for some time, measuring her, and then he shook his head. "Not as quickly anyway." He sighed, and then let slip a smile. "I see what you're doing," he said, "but Martin's not operating within the law."

"He's helping us," Katie said. "Everything we've asked of him—"

Reed clapped Katie on the shoulder and shook his head. "It's not up to me," he said. "You're arguing with the wrong person. But, for what it's worth, I'm just as much a fan as you are." He turned to watch Hart march Meg down the room and out into chill darkness beyond. "You did good work, Katie."

"Thank you, sir."

"We've still got to get this sorted out, to the satisfaction of Drake and Dora, but it shouldn't take too long. I'll have Craig book us a flight home. You want tonight or tomorrow?"

"Tonight!" She said it almost before he could finish the question, and he chuckled.

"You got it." He glanced back over his shoulder, toward Eric's corner, and then nodded that direction. "I think your grateful citizen has a few more words for you." He saw the hesitation in Katie's eyes, and his smile broadened. "Okay, people," he called out in a bellow that filled the room, "let's clear it out. We'll put this place under lock-down, and you can come back for any evidence you need later. Move it!" He started walking slowly toward the door, shepherding the police ahead of him, chiding them along more through personality than real authority. Katie watched him with a smile.

Then, as the door fell shut, she turned back to Theresa, and felt her smile fade.

15. Expectation

The sound of the door's locks engaging echoed in the room's sudden silence. Theresa stood by Eric's side, some ten steps away from Katie, and they stood with eyes locked for a long moment, in total silence.

Theresa broke the moment with a brief embarrassed smile as she looked down. Katie quickly crossed the distance and caught Theresa's hands, earning her another smile.

"You did it," Theresa said without looking up. Her voice held quiet awe. "You broke through all the silence, all the secrecy."

"I had help," Katie said, tucking a lock of her hair behind her ear. "It wasn't all me—"

"It was you," Theresa said earnestly. "It was you who came through that door, Katie. It was you who faced her down, all by yourself."

"I couldn't bring a crowd," Katie said, and Theresa finally met her eyes with a laughing grin.

"That's exactly what I mean," she said. "You didn't give up, you didn't back down in pursuit of justice for Eric...." A sigh escaped her, but she shook it off. "And then you did so much more to protect his legacy."

Katie blushed. "I'm not a hero Mrs. Barnes. I understand the importance of Gevia."

Theresa's lips quirked up, and she shrugged. "It's more important to us than most." She stepped back and took Eric's hand. Katie had to fight the urge to look away.

She didn't hide it is as well as she'd hoped, because Theresa cocked her head in curiosity then gasped a tiny, "Oh!" She went back to Katie and caught her eyes. "How long has it been?"

Katie said, "I don't know what you mean." She gave herself the lie, though, by wiping tears from her eyes. She blinked them away then forced a brave smile.

Theresa took Katie's hands now. "Where is your father?"

"He's in Boston," Katie said with a sniffle. "It's a very good facility...."

"Good," Theresa said. "That's great." She paused, then asked again. "How long has it been since you went to see him?"

"I haven't...." Katie had to wipe her eyes again. "I talk to him. I call and tell him about my life. Almost every day."

"Over Hathor?" she asked, and Katie nodded. Theresa said, "Then you never get to see him, to hold his hand...."

"I *can't*!" Katie said. "I don't understand how you do it." She sniffed. "I don't understand how my mom does it either."

"It's love," Theresa said, with a sad smile for Katie. "The same thing that makes it hard for you, actually. He needs me now, more than ever." She turned tender eyes on her stricken husband. "And I still need him. All the time." She brushed his face gently with her fingertips, reminding Katie of her mom at her father's bedside.

"Eight...eight years," Katie said. When Theresa looked back Katie looked away. "It's been a long time."

"And yet he's still there," Theresa said. "He can still be in your life, Katie."

"No." Katie wiped her eyes. "I walked away. I moved on."

"You didn't," Theresa tilted Katie's chin up to meet her eyes. "Not if you still call him. Not if you still care this much." She smiled. "You've been there for him, all this time, without taking the comfort of seeing him still alive—"

"But he's not," Katie said, more harshly than she meant to. "He won't ever be again. It hurts too much to pretend. I'm sorry." She looked at Eric and shook her head. "I don't mean to be cruel, but that's all it is. Pretending."

Katie expected anger or hurt, but all she saw in the other woman's eyes was sympathy. The silence stretched, and then Theresa gave Katie a quick, tight hug. She stepped away afterward, clearly embarrassed, and fixed her eyes on Eric. "He taught me a lot of things," she said, then chuckled. "A lot of things. But one of the most important things I've learned in all these years is not to underestimate the *power* of human expectation." She squeezed Katie's hand, unashamed now, and smiled with sincerity as her eyes roamed the dark tables of the lab. "We can work miracles, Katie. I've seen it."

Katie had no answer for that, and Theresa seemed to understand. She turned away again, leaving Katie some time to compose herself. Katie dried her eyes and caught her breath, but she still felt out of order. She straightened her clothes and adjusted her hair. At last she couldn't put it off any longer. She went to stand by Theresa's side and forced herself to look at Eric's serene face. The machines hummed and glowed, eerie guardian angels in the scientist's strange tomb. Katie's heart beat faster but it didn't race. She took a deep breath and let it out slowly. There was no need to run. There was just a man, asleep in his bed.

"I know you're right," Katie said at last. "I should...I mean, I ought to—"

"Hush, now," Theresa said, her voice comforting. "We've said enough about that." She sighed. "I guess you need to go."

"No," Katie said, then she sighed too. "Well, yes. I do." She looked over her shoulder at the exit, imagining all the hubbub in the grounds outside. "It's just so quiet here."

Theresa nodded. "It's peaceful here. It's a nice place to rest." She sighed. "I...I don't know what will happen now."

"We'll take care of it," Katie said, making a promise on Martin's behalf. "After everything you've given—"

"Enough about that, too," she said. "Whatever happens, we gave our best."

Katie nodded. "He changed the world."

The other woman smiled, and Katie knew she wasn't thinking about Gevia—about the lies and the secrets, about sacrifices and mistakes. She was thinking about a young man in a cramped apartment, asleep on their couch with all the wisdom of the age spread out in the pages around him, and a new idea blooming in his dreams. She was thinking about the man who cured cancer. "He changed the world," she said, pride rich in her voice. "And he loved me."

Katie squeezed her hand. She drew away, then stopped. "I really should go—"

"Of course!" she said earnestly. "Don't let me keep you."

"But we'll be in touch," Katie said. She withdrew another step. "If you need anything...."

Theresa met her eyes, that smile still there, and said softly, "Go. Live your life."

Katie went. Her footsteps rang loud in the cavernous silence and the room behind her felt empty. Alone. The feeling of a tomb came to her again, and she shivered. She had an urge to look back, to make sure the man and woman in the corner were really there, but she couldn't make herself do it. She couldn't quite catch her breath, either, until the door fell heavily shut behind her.

A police officer stood waiting in the lobby, one of Dora's with the look of a rookie about him. He glanced up as soon as Katie came through the door, and then rushed to her. "Agent Pratt," he said, "I'm supposed to tell you Agent Reed is in the administrative building and—"

"Take him a message," Katie said, cutting him off. "Tell him I'll see him at the airport. I'm done here."

The officer blinked in surprise, but Katie didn't give any more explanation. She pushed through the door and past the knot of other officers—police and military alike—arguing with Dora Hart about some matter of policy on the lawn. There were onlookers, too. There were always onlookers. This time it was a crowd of researchers and medical staff, gathered at a respectful distance, pointing and whispering among themselves, and Katie took a moment to consider how strange that building must be to all of them. Until she and Reed had come, the laboratory doors had only ever opened for three other people. These men and women had the clearance necessary to work in one of the last restricted areas in the nation, and yet this building right next door to theirs was a complete mystery to them. Katie could only imagine the rumors tonight would spawn.

She shook her head at the thought, as she slipped through the iron gates and out onto the street. There would be rumors, as sure as there were onlookers. Before she got back to her hotel room there would be stories flying about Eric, about Meg, about Gevia. None of it would be true—not yet—but then, nothing about Gevia was true. It was all a fragile web of lies, so easy to break—

A voice called out her name, drawing her out of her thoughts. She looked up the street, and heard it again. It was a car parked on the curb, waiting to give her a ride. She approached it with a look of sheer curiosity, and pulled the door open to find a route back to her hotel room already prepped on the driver's monitor. She climbed in and let out a tired sigh as the door fell closed. Then she whispered quietly, "God bless you, Martin Door."

She half expected him to answer, some clever comment or humble deflection, but there was only silence. That was enough to suit her. She sank back into the soft chair and closed her eyes. Reed would probably be irritated at her for disappearing, but she didn't have the stomach to wrap things up—to sort out the politics and the permissions with the lieutenant and Chief Hart. She didn't want to face Meg again, either. She wanted to go home.

She didn't notice it happening, but she fell asleep before the car got to her hotel. The driver had to *bing* twice to wake her up, and she was still groggy on the elevator ride up to her room. She had a fleeting, horrible fear that maybe she, too, had been drugged. It had certainly been the girl's intention. But in this case it was something far more straightforward. She was exhausted, and now that all the anxiety of the investigation was gone she was crashing. She'd always done that, at the close of a big case. All her life. She made it to her room, closed the door behind her, and fell face-first onto the bed. It was everything she could do to keep from falling asleep for the night.

Instead she measured her breathing, and ran through everything she needed to take care of. It was a short list. Her bags were still mostly packed, but she needed to grab her dirty clothes from yesterday and the toiletries from the bathroom. Reed was arranging their transport, but she needed to figure out exactly when and where, and somehow be awake to get there. She should make a pot of coffee, she decided, but instead of getting up and doing that, she stared at the print on the blanket from half an inch away.

She should call Reed. If he was at the Administrative Building, they could get a message through to him. She should try to explain, make sure he didn't need her back there. At the very least she should check in with Craig, see if she had any business messages. Without getting up, she said tiredly, "Hathor, connect me to Dad. Thanks." It buzzed and buzzed, and then asked her if she wanted to leave a message. There was a sudden weight on her chest and she had to fight to draw a breath, but she managed and forced out the word, "Yes." Then she had to go through it all again, to get enough air to say, "Dad.... I love you, Dad. I'm going to come see you. Soon." She cried then, for real. All the tears she'd held back at the clinic, all the emotion she'd battled every time she'd been there. Everything that had been building for two days came pouring out of her, and she let it go.

When it was over, when she was finally catching her breath again and dabbing her tears dry with a cheap tissue from the hotel's nightstand, she heard a voice over her headset. "Hi, Katie." It was Martin. "That was sweet."

She gasped, horrified at the interruption, and he clearly understood. "I'm sorry," he said. "I didn't mean to pry. I wasn't trying to be.... Look, I'm sorry." His breath escaped him. "I just needed to talk to you, and I was waiting for a good time."

"In the cab would have been better."

She heard him smile. "I didn't want to wake you." She shook her head, irritated, but he went on. "I need to thank you, Katie. Even more than Theresa did. You did so much to protect my work—"

"I need you," Katie said simply. She made her tone cruel. "That's all there is to it. I need you. Mrs. Barnes tried to convince me I was a hero, but I would have done nothing here without your help. I would have done nothing with Janeane's case, either, if it hadn't been for you." She shook her head. "I can't afford to say no to you."

"You're hurting," Martin said, gently chiding, "and you're being pretty hard on yourself. I saw what you did for Janeane, and I saw what you did for Theresa, here. And what you did for me. You risked your life keeping Reed out of it, Katie. You didn't have to do that." He sighed. "I'm not a mercenary. No, I'm not prepared to hand myself over to the FBI, but you have to believe me. I'm here for you. As much as I can be. You don't have to do special favors just to make that happen." He was silent for a moment, but Katie had nothing to say. After a while he said, "I owe you, Katie. If I didn't already, I certainly do now. I am in your debt."

"No," she said, flustered, but he spoke over her.

"And I have something for you, too. A token." He went on quickly. "I don't mean we're even. I'm not even sure this is something you want to know. But I found something...."

"What?"

"It's about your father," he said. "It's about his condition."

"Don't," she said softly, but he didn't hear her whisper.

"He was one of the five cases. The same drug that Meg used on Eric. I got into the sealed records, Katie, and his name was at the top of the list." She sat on the edge of the bed, her eyes closed, and said nothing. New tears burned in her eyes, but she didn't have much more left to give. Concerned, Martin said, "Katie?"

"I'm here," she said. "It...it doesn't change anything."

"I know," he said. "I just thought you would want to know."

"Thank you." She sniffled, and wiped her cheek with the crumpled tissue. "Thank you, Martin." She couldn't force any emotion into her voice.

"Umm...it's nothing." He sounded as awkward as she felt. "Hey, uh, I need to go. I want to help out some with the people who were trying to contact Miss Cohn. But I'll be in touch—"

"Yeah," Katie said. "Later."

For a moment he said nothing, then quietly, "Goodbye, Katie."

She spoke a command to turn off the room's lights, and for a long time she just sat there, in the silence and the darkness, alone with her thoughts. The next time her headset buzzed, nearly an hour later, she rose mechanically and went to grab her handheld from the nightstand. It showed her a travel itinerary warning, letting her know she needed to be at the airport in twenty minutes. She pressed the button to call for a cab, then moved into the bathroom to gather her things.

Five minutes later she was at the curb, and in fifteen she was at the airport. She waited alone in the boarding area until another buzz and another message on the handheld directed her through the boarding gate and onto her flight. She picked a seat by the window and sat staring out into the dark night while other passengers took their places.

She startled awake at a thud as Reed threw his bag into the overhead bin. The window's chill felt sharp against her forehead, and the soft little noises of passengers settling into their seats felt eerily exaggerated all around her. She blinked at Reed as he fell into the seat next to her. Then he turned to her.

"Oof," he said, shaking his head. "You look exhausted."

"I am exhausted," she said. "Can we go home?"

He smiled at her and almost patted her knee. "We can go home," he said. "We're heading there now." He pressed back in his chair, and pulled out his handheld. "Why don't you get some sleep on the flight? I'll get us checked back in at home."

She turned her head his way, curious what exactly he was working on, but couldn't quite focus on the screen. Before the plane ever left the ground, she was asleep again.

In DC, Reed woke her with a gentle touch on her arm. He spoke her name softly in her ear and she smiled, climbing slowly out of a dreamless rest, then stretched lazily and looked around the plane. Apart from the two of them, it was empty.

She looked to Reed, uncomprehending, and he smiled back. There was a sadness in his eyes that he tried to hide. "Good morning, Agent Pratt."

"Morning?" Katie said. "Really?"

He winced. "Only technically."

She gestured at the empty seats. "What's going on?"

"I exercised my special executive authority to buy you a few more minutes' rest."

"You shouldn't have," Katie said. "I'll be much more comfortable at home in bed."

That brought back the smile. And the sadness. He looked away. "We're not going home. Not yet."

Katie felt a black weight settle on her chest. She took a deep breath, trying to shake the feeling, and let it out in a sigh. "Accountability?"

"That's right. They've got some questions." She groaned, but he was watching her with too much concern, and there really wasn't any getting around it. "Fine. Let's get it over with."

He nodded and climbed from his seat.

Katie followed him, down the empty rows, through the empty gate, and out into a concourse that was still bustling, even at this time of night. She moved mechanically, dragging her bag behind her, and let Reed pick their path. He had a car waiting for them by the curb, and they rode most of the way to the office in silence.

Nearly there, he broke the silence. "Oh, hey, I got your message. Back at the clinic? It's no problem you heading out like that."

She frowned at him, confused, and he shrugged. "I just wanted to let you know that. Whatever else we've got waiting for us, I understand what happened after the bust. Meg gave us a pretty good account of what went on in there, and Mrs. Barnes corroborated it point for point. We got what we needed, and after what you went through, I wouldn't have expected you to hang around." He patted her knee. "I'm just glad you made it through."

She arranged her face into something like a smile for him. "Thanks," she said, and then the silence came back.

The building was mostly dark when they stepped out of the car. The lights in Rick's office upstairs stood out sharply against the blackness all around, and Katie and Reed both stood transfixed for a moment.

Then he took her hand and pulled her toward the doors. The lobby was empty, the elevator ride miserably quiet, but he didn't let her hand go until the elevator doors opened on their floor. Then he pulled the door open for her, and Katie gave him another smile.

The Steves were waiting for them. Stephen Penn had his back to the windows, waiting patiently in one of the guest chairs, but Steve Fredrik was in Rick's old throne, feet propped up on the desk while he read a report off a tablet-sized handheld. He set it aside as Katie approached and met her eyes with a glare.

"Thank you for joining us, Agent Pratt," he said. "That makes things much easier. Agent Reed, please place her under arrest."

From his place by the door, Stephen Penn shook his head. "Is that really necessary?"

At the same time, Reed stepped in front of Katie. "Not a chance," he barked.

Fredrik arched an eyebrow at Reed, then addressed his answer to his companion. "It's absolutely necessary. You saw as much I did, every minute since they left. She's been insubordinate, obstructing her own investigation and participating in the destruction of evidence. And worst of all, *after* we impressed upon her the seriousness of the crime, she's been willfully colluding with Martin Door."

"You're wrong," Reed said. "Katie is personally responsible for solving the investigation. And Martin Door isn't a criminal."

Fredrik showed his teeth. "Oh, he is now. Thanks to Katie, we've got enough evidence to bring the same charges against him. As soon as she's dealt with, catching Martin Door is going to be this office's highest priority."

Reed smirked. "It's not."

"Actually," Penn said with a tired sigh, "it is. We understand it won't be *your* highest priority—"

"Ah," Reed said. "I see."

Katie shook her head. "I don't. Reed's done nothing wrong—"

"Everything about this investigation has been a farce," Fredrik snapped. "From the moment you two picked it for a fun little field trip to the *vast* resources Reed expended chasing down your theories. You can't really tell me this little adventure is the right way to do business? The whole case could have been resolved from here, with a little bit of patience and a little more attention to detail—"

"And Theresa Barnes would be dead right now," Katie said. And Gevia's secret would be out. She didn't say that, though. She didn't want these men investigating the dark corners of Gevia.

Reed wasn't so careful. "This isn't even about the murder. The poisonings! In the course of this investigation—*because of* Katie's special resources—we were able to uncover a plot to sell national secrets—"

"Were you?" Penn asked, climbing to his feet. "See...we've been examining the events of the last twenty-four hours, and it seems like your investigation of Ellie Cohn fell apart. Maybe I'm missing something, but according to your records, she didn't turn out to be a threat at all."

Katie frowned. "What?" All eyes turned to her, and she shook her head. "No, that's not right. He—we found her buyers."

Fredrik favored her with a cruel little smile and shook his head. "Funny," he said. "I'd expect a detail like that to be entered in your casefile. Your man Reed was awfully careful to put in everything else."

She rounded on Reed, astonished, but he just gave a helpless little shrug. He seemed as surprised by the outburst as the other two.

"I don't understand!" she said.

And then Martin spoke into her ear. "Give it a moment," he said.

She opened her mouth to shout at him, to demand an explanation, but in front of these two men she didn't dare. She ground her teeth, acid roiling in her stomach, and watched as Fredrik pulled his feet off the desk with a slow melodrama and unfolded himself in front of her.

"What you need to understand," he said, "is that you're through playing games with the mission and resources of this department. Miss Pratt—"

"Hold on," Penn said. That drew an irritated frown from Fredrik, but the other auditor ignored him, one hand to his headset as he listened to something. "All right," he said after a moment. "Put this call on the room's speakers."

Another voice spoke into the room. "That's a fine idea," it said. It was an older man's voice, rich with authority, and Katie saw a surprised frown crease Fredrik's forehead. At the same time, the corner of Reed's mouth ticked up in a victorious smile.

"Mr. Director," he said. "Good to hear from you."

"Thank you, Reed. Sorry I couldn't intervene sooner."

"Intervene?" Fredrik said. He had his aplomb back, and he showed it with a contemptuous smile. "Under the circumstances, you don't have any authority to intervene here. This is our investigation. Contact Senator Bruin—"

"I'm here," came another man's voice, this one irritated and tired, and Fredrik's face fell again. "And you're done," the senator went on. "This investigation is over."

"What?" Fredrik snapped. "But we've *got* them. We've got them both. I didn't even get to Reed's misdeeds—"

"Reed is a fine agent," Bruin said, as though reading it off a card. The words were hollow. "And the president has made it clear—"

"The president?" Fredrik said. "What does he have to do with it."

The director answered him with considerably more sincerity than the senator had managed. "He understands the importance of Gevia to this nation and its people."

"And that's precisely why it was a high crime to let this girl play fast and loose with such a critical investigation—"

The director spoke right over him. "And that's precisely why it was so important to remove the identities of Ellie Cohn's buyers from the casefile report," he said. "Katie Pratt *did* track that down—"

"I added it under your name," Martin whispered in her ear.

"And we pulled it almost immediately, but it was exactly what we needed. We picked up two Chinese nationals with ghosted identities at a Canadian border crossing two hours ago."

"You can connect them Ellie Cohn?" Reed said.

Katie could hear the director's smile in his answer. "That we did, but we're going to need your help to nail down the actual conspiracy charge."

Reed smiled back. "I'll get right on it, sir."

"I promised the president as much," the director said.

"You can't just let this go!" Fredrik shouted. "This woman colluded with Martin Door—"

"We know about Martin Door," the director said, and though he kept his tone even it was clear he was losing his patience. "It's our considered opinion—mine and the president's—that Mr. Door proved to be an invaluable special informant in Katie's investigation. She's to be commended for utilizing him so effectively."

"But, but—" Fredrik stammered, and Senator Bruin cut him off.

"Forget it, Fredrik." He sounded tired, and more bored than disappointed. "They've got you all tied up."

The director sighed. "Your investigation's over. Now. The office still wants to hear your official report, but you're done interfering with this team's work. Understood?" He didn't even wait for answer. "Katie, Reed...good work, both of you. You're national heroes. Reed, I'll be in touch." With that, he dropped from the line.

Fredrik was still sitting in the chair, stunned. All eyes fell on him, and after a moment he pulled himself up. Fire flashed in his eyes. "That's not the end of it," he said. "I've got evidence—"

"Give it up," Penn said. He stepped up to Reed and extended a hand with an air of great professionalism. "Thank you for your cooperation in this matter."

Reed shook it, with just the hint of a sarcastic smile, and nodded back. Penn tipped his head to Katie, too, then left the room. Fredrik looked helplessly after the other, then turned his hateful gaze to Reed and Katie.

Katie jerked her head toward the door. "You heard the man," she said. "Hit the road. We've got work to do, and you're sitting in my boss's chair."

THE END

Don't miss out!

Click the button below and you can sign up to receive emails whenever Aaron Pogue publishes a new book. There's no charge and no obligation.

Did you love *Expectation*? Then you should read *Restraint* by Aaron Pogue!

We abandoned privacy and turned databases into something like gods. They listened to our prayers. They met our needs and blessed us with new riches. They watched over us, protected us, and punished the wicked. We almost made a paradise.

But there were those who tried to hide from the databases' all-seeing eye. They used their wealth or power or intellect to turn themselves into ghosts within the endless archive. The FBI's Ghost Targets team became experts at tracking them down, and they threw the worst of the monsters into private prisons where even Hathor's eyes could not see.

Now a new threat forces Katie Pratt to enter the dark halls of one of these prisons. An old adversary trapped in Shadow Mountain holds the key to the mystery, and he'll only give it to Katie. But when a Shadow Mountain contractor is murdered, his hidden execution uncovers the most advanced ghosting device ever created. Katie must solve the murder to save Hathor, and she will have to face down wardens, politicians, mob bosses, and deadly ghosts to do it. Only then will she uncover the terrifying secrets locked up in Shadow Mountain.

Restraint is the third book in the Ghost Targets series.

Read more at AaronPogue.com.

Also by Aaron Pogue

A Consortium of Worlds
A Consortium of Worlds No. 1
A Consortium of Worlds No. 2

A Dragonswarm Short Story
Remnant
From Embers

Auric's Valiants
Notes from a Thief
Auric and the Wolf

Ghost Targets
Surveillance
Expectation
Restraint
Camouflage

The Dragonprince's Arrows
A Darkness in the East

The Dragonprince's Legacy
Taming Fire
The Dragonswarm
The Dragonprince's Heir
The Original Dragonprince Trilogy

Unstressed Syllables Presents
Turn Your Story into an eBook: Easy Self-Publishing with
Draft2Digital.com

Watch for more at AaronPogue.com.

About the Author

Aaron Pogue is a husband and a father of two who lives in Oklahoma City, OK. Aaron started writing at the age of ten. His first novels were high fantasy set in the rich world of the FirstKing, but he's explored mainstream thrillers, urban fantasy, and several kinds of science fiction. Author of the Dragonprince's Legacy, the Godlanders War, and the Ghost Targets series, Aaron Pogue has sold a quarter of a million books since his debut in 2010.

Aaron has been a Technical Writer with the Federal Aviation Administration and a writing professor at the university level. He holds a Master of Professional Writing degree from the University of Oklahoma. He also serves as the President of Draft2Digital, an ebook formatting, conversion, and distribution service that he helped found in 2012.

Read more at AaronPogue.com.